RAIDER TO THE RESCUE!

Raider moved up to them from below their feet, straddling their legs and cold-cocking the brave with the butt of his Colt. The Indian sighed as he lost consciousness. Raider was pulling him off her when she realized what had happened. She started to scream; he hit her with his fist to shut her up. She lay limp as a cotton doll.

She was naked. He couldn't take her without something to cover her. He fumbled about in the darkness and after what seemed a half an hour found her clothes. He had gotten on her mocassins and was about to pick her up when a familiar voice spoke.

"Stop. Put her down..." At that moment the overcast parted, revealing the full moon. Its light silvered the blade in Crazy Horse's rising hand...

Other books in the RAIDER series by
J. D. HARDIN

RAIDER
SIXGUN CIRCUS
THE YUMA ROUNDUP
THE GUNS OF EL DORADO
THIRST FOR VENGEANCE
DEATH'S DEAL
VENGEANCE RIDE
CHEYENNE FRAUD
THE GULF PIRATES
TIMBER WAR
SILVER CITY AMBUSH
THE NORTHWEST RAILROAD WAR
THE MADMAN'S BLADE
WOLF CREEK FEUD
BAJA DIABLO
STAGECOACH RANSOM
RIVERBOAT GOLD
WILDERNESS MANHUNT
SINS OF THE GUNSLINGER

BLACK HILLS TRACKDOWN

BERKLEY BOOKS, NEW YORK

BLACK HILLS TRACKDOWN

A Berkley Book/published by arrangement with
the author

PRINTING HISTORY
Berkley edition/February 1989

All rights reserved.
Copyright © 1989 by J.D. Hardin
This book may not be reproduced in whole or in part,
by mimeograph or any other means, without permission.
For information address: The Berkley Publishing Group,
200 Madison Avenue, New York, NY 10016.

ISBN: 0-425-11399-X

A BERKLEY BOOK ® TM 757,375
Berkley Books are published by the Berkley Publishing Group,
200 Madison Avenue, New York, NY 10016
The name "BERKLEY" and the "B" logo
are trademarks belonging to the Berkley Publishing Corporation.

PRINTED IN THE UNITED STATES OF AMERICA

10 9 8 7 6 5 4 3 2 1

CHAPTER ONE

Why the six bad apples had taken the trouble to blow the express car door clean off its hinges Raider couldn't figure, but this they'd done and were now inside, holding the two clerks at bay and pouring forth a hailstorm of lead in the direction of the three Pinkertons.

"Lousy friggin' odds," muttered Raider, squeezing himself tight behind the base of a tree as best he could to deny the outlaws a target. Supporting himself on one elbow, he thumbed cartridges into chambers, then gingerly ran a finger down the top of the barrel of his Peacemaker. "Hot and gettin' hotter..."

He snaked his iron around the tree trunk and took a quick look, inviting two shots which whistled by, perilously close to his head. But not before he got off two of his own. The first bit the right side of the door jamb four inches from a jowly, red-faced snake peering out above a filthy-looking, bearded man wielding a sawed-off 10-gauge. Filthy Beard was more careful than Red Face. Raider's second shot confirmed it. The bullet caught the topmost miscreant full in the right cheek, driving into his skull. He fell like a pillar, his gun dropping from his grasp and landing on the gravel below. The three outlaws crowding the opposite jamb roared in chorus and emptied their guns at Raider's tree, almost as if they were trying to shoot through it to get at him. As luck would have it, they finished throwing their loads at just about the same time. Hubert Fisk, one of the other Pinkerton operatives, crouching behind a rock about thirty feet to Raider's right, had the best angle, and was quick to take advantage of the outlaws' temporary helplessness. He emptied his gun at them and killed one; painfully wounded a second, putting a slug deep into his arm; and sent the third man scurrying for better cover.

"Good shootin', Hubie!" boomed Raider, grinning and waving, then cursing as Filthy Beard fired and hit Fisk squarely in the neck. Blood spurted from his throat, his smile of triumph darkened, his eyes swiveled in his head, and down he went.

"My God, my God..." rasped Operative Lydell Ormsby, bellied down in a small depression to Raider's left.

"Pull down, you asshole!" snapped Raider.

Ormsby did so, just in time. A wedge of lead whined straight through the space vacated by his handsome face two seconds before. Raider liked Fisk, and his death shocked him. He should remember that pain and death went with the territory, he thought, only you never did get used to the sight of a fellow operative gunned down. Fisk had been guilty of a basic tactical error, an understandable human error, but one every man worth the salt in his blood had to be wary of when the guns started going off. If you spot an advantage, one that prompts you to empty your weapon, and you hit your enemy, *don't react to it*. Don't let down your guard, don't take a good look and thereby expose yourself. Proud as you may be, save it for later. Fisk had stayed up a whisker too long to savor his triumph. It was only human, but it was careless and it had killed him.

Raider glanced Ormsby's way. Fisk he liked, Ormsby he did not. He was a loudmouth, a braggart, a know-it-all; he was constantly, incessantly correcting people. He had a mouth and a manner that invited deep and abiding resentment.

"Asshole is what he is," muttered Raider.

If he had a choice, he'd be on this job alone. Out of better than two hundred operatives he was the only one that Allan Pinkerton permitted to operate solo. Raider'd had a partner for years—Doc Weatherbee—but Doc was retired from the agency, had a wife and was working at a nine-to-five job. They'd tried to give Raider other partners after Doc—half a dozen at least—but it never worked out and he thought that the Chicago office had finally given up.

Until this assignment. Billy Pinkerton, in charge of the Denver office, had talked him into joining the team of Fisk and Ormsby on a U.P. case. The Union Pacific was the agency's number-one client and Billy; his father, Allan Pinkerton; and William Wagner, the old man's long-time super-in-charge in Chicago doubled over backward for the line. Raider had always figured that the railroad needed the agency a lot more than the agency needed the U.P.'s business, but Allan Pinkerton pooh-poohed this attitude. In any event, the bunch inside the car—what was left of them, Raider figured three, counting the one too severely wounded to be any further threat—had already knocked over two trains and were in the process of ransacking this one when he, Fisk, and Ormsby caught up with them. Curiously, the outlaws only had eyes for the express safe and the mailbags; they had no interest in the passengers.

The Pinkertons had ridden long and hard in pursuit of them. All the way from Maple Hill in Pottawotamie County, a good eighty miles to the west. The outlaws had no idea they were being followed. They'd tracked them all the way to this spot, about a mile from Cartwood to the east, where they'd stopped the train by piling rocks on the tracks, and at the moment were attempting to turn over the express car.

The Pinkertons had followed them with Raider and Ormsby arguing every mile. Raider was all for catching up and having it out before they struck a third time. Ormsby wanted to catch them in the act. Fisk, as easy-going as any operative Raider had ever ridden with, was happy to do either. Raider was by nature as stubborn as a goat. Ormsby was even stubborner. Raider contended that there was no need to catch them in the act since they already had the goods on them for the first two jobs. Why risk clerks' and passengers' lives in another go-round? Side by side they had followed the tracks east, skillfully keeping their quarry within sight without being spotted themselves, arguing, insulting each other, threatening, sniping. Ormsby finally got his way only because Raider gave up.

Now it had come down to three against two with something of a Mexican standoff threatening. The outlaws had the protection of the car, the Pinkertons that of the landscape. Both sides' horses, meanwhile, wandered freely about in the woods. Raider pictured his roan mare traipsing all the way to Kansas City by the time everybody's ammunition gave out.

He sneaked a look and got off two wild shots at Filthy Beard who by now had lowered himself to the floor and was peering around the lower right hand corner of the doorway. He was still being sensibly careful. One of Raider's slugs found the edge of the floor. An inch higher and it would have caught his target smack in the top of the sternum.

"Shit . . ."

He'd emptied his gun again. He felt his belt for cartridges. Twice around his fingers traveled. Again he cursed; he found only four. He glanced over at Fisk's bleeding remains. He did not wear a cartridge belt, preferring to carry his ammunition in its pasteboard box in the side pocket of his jacket. He had taken out the box and dumped its contents by his left hip. The shell casings gleamed like bits of gold in the late afternoon sun. Raider licked his lips. Then turned the other way.

"Ormsby. . ." he whispered loudly. "Hey, pssst . . ."

The object of his attention turned and looked.

"What's the matter now."

"Shut up and listen, Chrissakes. Pay 'tention. I wan'cha' t' cover me."

"Cover?"

"I'm gonna squirm over an' get Hubert's ammo. Better yet, make a run for it, it can't be more'n ten yards."

"Are you insane? They'll pot you before you take three steps. It's wide open all the way, not a tree, not even a stump. How in heaven's name did you run out of ammunition?"

"I been shootin', goddammit. Just keep 'em busy ten seconds. Cover me. You know how to cover somebody, don'cha?"

"It's suicide. Go ahead, this I've got to see."

"You gonna cover me or not?"

"You're crazy! You wouldn't dare, even *you* wouldn't be that stupid . . ."

Raider stared at him long and hard before turning right for another look at his objective. A stare that announced most eloquently "do it and do it right or I'll kill you!"

Away he sprang like a runner out of the starting blocks. As in most such situations, everything that could happen happened at once. A second or two elapsed before the outlaws' eyes conveyed what was happening to their brains and their brains signaled their muscles. Raider covered a good third of the distance before they began shooting. Lead bracketed him, thudded into the ground and passed through one side of him and his ducked head several times in his imagination. He did not look toward the car; his head was actually turned slightly toward the deeper woods stretching behind Fisk's body and to his own right. His right ear was tuned to Ormsby's cover fire.

Only he heard none. Not a single shot.

"Sonovabitch bastard!"

He couldn't believe it. As he pressed on, crouched low, deliberately shifting his upper body up and down to make of himself a harder target, he turned to look behind him at Ormsby. He sighted him up to his neck in his hole-cover staring at him with a look of absolute wonderment on his face. As if he didn't believe his eyes. Raider exploded with anger, cursed him, cursed his mother, and dove for the rock. He landed behind it, but not before a ricochet caught him low down the ladder of his ribs, while an undeflected shot got him in the upper arm.

He shook off both pains, knowing from experience that as bad as they were, they'd be worse shortly. Positioned over Fisk's prostrate body behind the rock, he began sweeping the scattered cartridges toward him with one hand. Three separate shots threatened to sever his hand from his wrist, but he managed to scoop most of the shells close to him without being hit a third time. He fumbled six into his gun, cursing, looking over at Ormsby now twice the distance from him.

"Why the hell didn't you cover me, you asshole! Sonovabitch. I oughta blow your head off, Chrissakes! Don't think I ain't gonna report this in the goddamn report; op'rative's s'posed t' cover his sidekick every time, all the time. Some goddamn Pink you turned out. What the hell you ever sign on in the first place for, you're the worse damn..."

He stopped short, realizing he was talking to a dead man. He stared at him. Ormsby did not move, did not alter the look of astonishment draping his features. Raider saw no blood. He didn't have to, he could recognize death; he'd seen it so often.

"Jus' as well, asshole; saves me beatin' you t' death after this shindig is over. Goddamn side... goddamn arm, damn!"

Neither wound was bleeding badly, nothing resembling Fisk's death wound in the throat.

"Let's get this crap over with and get me to a pill-roller!"

Again he cast a glance at Ormsby, figuring he'd probably caught his just before Raider went into his leap. He could be sure of one thing, his cover hadn't gotten off a single shot.

"Asshole..."

Something was going on inside the car. In the shadows he could see both clerks, visored and in their shirtsleeves, arms upraised.

Raider emitted a low whistle that combined surprise and elation.

"They must think it's all over. They got him an' Fisk an' think they got me."

They had to know they'd hit him and were evidently assuming they'd killed him. Even as this thought skimmed through his mind their actions reinforced it. One outlaw emerged from shadow and showed his back framed by the doorway. He stood with his gun holstered, his fists on his hips. Then he turned. Filthy Beard came up beside him while the third man continued to hold the two helpless clerks at bay. The outlaws' job was too easy, mused Raider, up to now not one passenger or crew member had interfered with them. He pictured the passengers cowering and waiting for it to end. Well, their wait was over!

"Hey!" he called.

The man in full view stiffened, his hand starting for his gun. The shot found his heart, leaving a gleaming red spot the size of a dime on his vest pocket. Raider shot the other in the face; the bullet shattered his jaw and plowed its way through the back of his throat. White-faced and confused, the third man's right arm showed out of the shadows, his gun muzzle dropping into position. Raider put two shots six inches to the right of it. The man screamed like a girl and fell forward, hanging his face over the edge of the floor and still clinging to his unfired gun.

Raider licked his bone-dry lips, tried and failed to clear his even dryer throat, and shifted his legs under the sheet of the hospital bed on which he sat, propped up by pillows. The hospital was in the small town of Cartwood, a tiny hospital with no more than ten beds. The overwhelmingly strong smell of ammonia nauseated him. He grimaced as the stench shot up his nostrils like twin needles and pricked his aching head. His left arm was in a sling. The doctor had dug out both slugs.

Dr. Thaddeus Milner stood smiling at him. He looked ancient. Raider guessed that he must be at least in his late eighties. No prune that ever dried was more shriveled. No starving Indian carried less meat on his bones. No eyes were weaker, floating watery and enormous behind spectacles nearly a half inch thick. No hair was wilder, not even Andy Jackson's.

"How we doing?" he asked good-naturedly.

"Shi..." began Raider, and caught himself mid-swear as Nurse Fidler, who was the size of a bale of cotton came sailing in.

She stood silently behind the doctor, and from the look of her glasses, Raider guessed that she was as blind as was the doctor.

"Lousy," said Raider.

"You have a visitor," said Dr. Milner, Cartwood's only practicing physician. As Nurse Fidler had said earlier, "You go to Doc Milner or go to the grave."

"I don't know anybody in this burg."

"He's from Kansas City. Mr. Allan Pinkerton . . ."

"Aw for Chris . . ."

Again he caught himself before he could finish. Nurse Fidler departed, returning seconds later with the chief in tow. Allan Pinkerton looked travel weary. The last Raider had heard he was leaving Chicago for New Orleans to attend a convention of private law-enforcement professionals. He beamed benevolently as he approached, offered his right hand, perceived that Raider's right arm was immobilized, switched to his left, and shook Raider's left.

"Only a few minutes now, remember," cautioned Dr. Milner.

"Oh baloney, you'd think I was at death's friggin' door. It's only a couple scratches."

Dr. Milner waved both hands, as if to dismiss not only sound but sight of him, and withdrew, shaking his head.

"Raider, if you don't look the wrath of Jehovah himself. Run down, peaked; I see by your eyes you've been drinking heavier than usual of late. Look at your skin, your flesh, especially around your mouth. Lost weight, too, and pale as a sheet. Of course you've lost blood, I'm sure, but wounds or no, I've never seen you look poorer."

"You don't look so great yourself, Mr. Pinkerton."

"Now, now, let's not get personal. How long do you think it'll be before you're back on your feet?"

"Jesus Christ, I just got here late last night. I'm weakern' a wet sock, I musta lost eight quarts o' friggin' blood. Both my wounds feel like he dug the slugs out with a round-point shovel. Got the touch of a friggin' gorilla. And look at this place, will ya? It'd make a better saloon than a friggin' hospital. These sheets don't smell too clean, neither. Get a whiff."

"All right, all right, all right, all right! Have mercy, man. I've no intention of tiring you out in your present condition to be sure, there's no need to question you about the shootout. I got it all from the two clerks, anyway. You emerged the shining hero of the piece again, so it seems."

"Better believe it. There was at least a dozen o' them against the three of us."

Pinkerton's face darkened. "Pity about Fisk and Ormsby. Which reminds me: I must contact Wagner when I get back to Kansas City before I continue on to New Orleans, get both men's home addresses so that I can write letters of condolence to their bereaved."

He shook his head and sighed. His reaction was genuine, Raider knew. Whenever an operative was killed in the line of duty he took it very personally and hard. As if every man was his son. They talked about the battle; Raider soon saw that he could add little to what the clerks had already reported. The money had been retrieved. The big bellies at U.P. headquarters in San Francisco were happy. Even if they were aware that two operatives had given their lives to get their money back, it wouldn't have dampened their pleasure. Money, money, he reflected, not only did it make the mare go, it ran the world, and human life and love and everything else was crowded into the back seat.

Dr. Milner stuck his head in. Pinkerton dutifully rose from his chair.

"May we have two more minutes, Doctor?"

Dr. Milner nodded and vanished.

"You shouldn't be down for more than a week or perhaps ten days, do you think?" From his expression, Pinkerton seemed somewhat self-conscious about voicing such a question.

"Three or four days."

"I wouldn't want you to rush things."

"Oh bullshit, if you wouldn't it'd be a friggin' first for sure."

"That's unfair, Raider."

"Truth can be. What's on your mind, anyhow?"

"Must something be on my mind? Must you imply I have an ulterior motive?"

"I don't know what in hell you're talkin' 'bout, but spit it out anyhow. I'm tired, I need my sleep."

"When you get out, when you're on your feet again and able to ride and use your. . . . Oh, it's your left arm that's wounded, not your right. That's good."

"What's good about it?"

"Your shooting hand and your arm are unscathed. Raider, have you ever heard me speak of Harmon W. Dubois?"

"No."

"We go back eons, Harmon and I. Back to Detroit when I started the agency and he was working in a local bank. He was instrumental in getting us our first contract. Harmon's semi-retired now, living in Kansas City with his wife, Velma. They have one son, Edgar. He's twenty-eight and married. President of the bank in Collardsville, Nebraska."

"I know the place, it's just down the line from Hot Springs, Dakota Terr'tory." He laughed and winced with the pain. "Ever tell you the story 'bout me an' the law in Hot Springs?"

"Another time. Listen. Last week—last Thursday as a matter of fact—Mrs. Dubois—her name is Adrienne, and quite a striking beauty she is, too—was out berrying. She was abducted by a passing party of Oglala Sioux."

"Crazy Horse . . ."

"Not him; that is we have no way of knowing it. Suffice to say, they're holding her prisoner. Her husband is beside himself. Harmon has asked for our help. He doesn't want to approach the army. He hesitates to approach the local law. What he wants—what he needs—is a lone operative, a man who knows the Oglalas, knows the area, can hunt them down, and rescue the poor woman, providing she's still alive."

"She is."

"You can bring it off, Raider, you're far and away the best man for this type of thing."

"Oh cut it out with the sugar-coated friggin' molasses, will ya? An' get somebody else. There's dozens o' guys. Contact Billy over in Denver, he'll getcha six. Besides, time's important, right? By the time I'm on my feet, four or five weeks from now, she could be long dead. Then too, Edgar won't wanna wait for me."

"You just finished saying she's in no danger."

"I didn't say no such thing, what I said was she's still alive. Injuns don't gen'rally kill womenfolk. They do worse. And if she's as good lookin' as you claim they'll likely do real worse."

"You said you think you'll be able to ride in three or four days. You can be in Collardsville in less than twenty hours if you take the train."

"I hate trains. You know I do. Can't stand 'em."

"A woman's life is at stake, Raider."

"Okay, okay. Don't pile it on."

"Then you'll do it?"

"What friggin' choice do I got?"

"Good man."

He lay a paternal hand against Raider's good shoulder and shook it gently.

"I'll be going. You get plenty of rest, get your strength back. I've already seen to all your bills. And when you get to Collardsville there'll be expense money waiting. You'll need a horse and gear." His smile weakened. "This is terribly important to me personally, Raider. Harmon is going through hell on earth. And her husband Edgar . . ."

"Yeah, yeah, yeah."

Once again Dr. Milner appeared at the door. Pinkerton said good-bye and left. Raider tried to sleep sitting up. He had almost dozed off when Milner's voice jolted him awake.

"I want you to get some sleep, do you hear me?"

"Jesus, you scared me. Why you gotta come sneakin' up on me like a damn raghead 'Pache? I'll sleep, but first I wanta look at my wounds. First the shoulder."

"Never mind, they're there, believe me."

"I wanta see what kinda job you did."

"I did a great job."

"Get the fat lady in here and just undo the bandage so's I can see."

"Never mind, damn it!"

"What are you gettin' so hot about? Wha'ja do, screw up?"

"You are something, you know that? You haven't even been here a full day yet, haven't been out from under the ether for more than six hours, and every minute you're grousing and grouching about something. You're loud, disturbing the other patients; demanding; brassy; argumentative. And the world's worst complainer!"

"I want t' see what you did! What the hell's so demandin' 'bout that?"

"Will you lower your voice!"

"You lower yours! What are you, 'shamed to show me what kinda' diggin' job you did? Is that it? You don't see too good, d'you, what d'you do, go in after a slug by feel?"

"Listen, plowboy..."

The word had a telling effect on Raider. He loathed and despised it. It conjured up disturbing visions of an illiterate Arkansas clodhopper, barefoot and stupid looking, chewing on a sprig of timothy, the eternal butt of city folks' jokes, a clown in bib overalls, a two-legged mule. Raider was originally from Fulton County, Arkansas, straight off the farm, finished with his schooling at the age of ten. The mere sound of the word plowboy made him see red, detonated his temper, ruptured his self-esteem. The doctor had no way of knowing this, had no inkling of the effect it would have on him. He found out.

"You horse's ass! You butcherin' pig! You wrinkled old, pill pushin', blind-eyed, mail-order sawbones, where you get off insultin' me? If you didn't have one foot in the grave, I'd bust your head in six places, you quack, you two-bit snake oil hornswoggler, voodoo witch doctor!"

"Get up. Get your clothes on, get out!"

"You bet your busted boots! I wouldn't stay six more seconds in this dump, this slaughterhouse fulla flies an' disease, stinkin' sheets, fat nurse can't hardly get through the door, can't see no bettern' you; Chrissakes, man's gotta be takin' 'is life in 'is hands t' go under your knife. Cleaver's more like it, pinch-point crowbar. How many poor sufferin' slobs you knock off this week?"

"Out! Your clothes and your property will be brought to you. Get dressed and leave the premises. And if you pass out at the front door, you'll lie there till the grackles peck you to the bone. I wash my hands of you!"

"'Bout time you washed your hands, you grubby old fraud!"

Raider dressed hurriedly and painfully. By virtue of sheer force of will combined with his blistering indignation he did not pass out at the front door. He nearly did, standing, his head spinning, his brain bouncing around inside it like the ball on a roulette wheel, but catching a cavernous breath, he managed to make it across the street and down the block to the Sunflower Saloon. He was lucky in that what could have been the more dangerous wound, the slug in his left side, had been a ricochet, and had not penetrated a fraction as deeply as the less dangerous, but more painful wound in his arm.

At the Sunflower he purchased two bottles of rye and carried them three doors back up the street to the hotel. The room he was given overlooked the street and the hospital across the way.

He sat by the open window, drinking and fuming, castigating all physicians and surgeons, all healers, setting those worthies who cut and draw chickens a sizable notch above them. He glanced back at the bed. He really should be in it, he thought, but not yet, not for a while. He had something he must do.

Dr. Milner came out, having finished for the day, just as Raider emptied the first bottle. He opened the window as wide as it would go, yelled down at him and hurled the empty. It missed by a wide margin, landing in the horse trough to Milner's left. The doctor looked up, scowled ferociously, and shook his fist.

"Quack!" Raider taunted.

"Plowboy!" Milner returned.

"Fraud! Butcher! Go home and wash out your friggin' conscience!"

CHAPTER TWO

Raider turned to doctoring himself, confident of his abilities, of his experience in the skill. He prescribed rye, dosing himself liberally with it every hour on the hour. Finishing the second bottle, he sent out for six more bottles.

He woke the following morning to discover his head displaced by an anvil. The blacksmith was hard at work *inside it,* hammering industriously, sending rhythmic shock waves of insidious pain to every corner of Raider's skull. The simple act of lifting his head from his pillow quadrupled the intensity of the blows and the agony they actuated. He lay without moving all morning long. Through the noon hour he lay motionless, and into the sultry afternoon. It was not until mid-afternoon that he was able to summon the strength to rise to a sitting position on the edge of the bed. The pain, meanwhile, had abated, his headache deserting his brain, descending his throat, settling in his stomach, rooting, growing, blossoming into nausea most wretched. He threw up several times.

At five o'clock he decided that the only way to dispatch his affliction would be to displace it with food. He tidied up as best he could, rinsed out his vomit-fouled mouth and went out for supper. He ate two steaks and three boiled spuds, returned to his room, threw them up and went back to bed.

He was asleep, dreaming of Dr. Milner. Raider had him tied to an operating table and was preparing to surgically remove his heart with a trowel when a loud knocking awoke him.

"Who the hell..."

It was about nine o'clock, not exactly the wee hours, but he'd been enjoying his dream and sleeping was good for him and being roused from it exceeded the cramped limits of his toleration.

He whipped open the door.

"What do ya mean wakin' a man outta a sound sleep..."

There stood a stranger, dressed expensively and in the height of fashion, from his shining top hat to his exorbitantly expensive imported Italian soft leather shoes. He wore white gloves, he carried an ivory-capped walking stick. He tipped his hat.

"Mr. Raider?"

"Who..."

"Edgar Dubois is the name. May I come in?"

In he sallied before Raider could respond, setting his hat on the washstand, leaning his stick against the wall, divesting himself of his cloak, folding it neatly, setting it at the foot of the bed, taking the solitary chair in which Raider had sat the day before tippling and waiting for Milner to come out. Raider noted, however, that while his visitor went through all these preparations for his visit, his handsome face betrayed little fondness for doing so. The stench of illness lingered in the little room and Dubois's expression belied his revulsion. He was not impressed by his host's choice of quarters. And not impressed by his host, who was disheveled, unshaven, and bleary-eyed; in short; the complete antithesis of the courageous knight errant Allan Pinkerton had limned in his mind's eye who was going to ride off and rescue his stolen wife.

"You're Operative Raider?" he asked, his tone skeptical.

"Hell yes. Little the worse for wear."

"Chief Pinkerton tells me that you were wounded."

"Couple o' scratches. I'm on the mend."

"Good."

Raider noticed that although his voice said it was, his face said it was the least of his concerns. Without being asked to do so, Dubois recapped the events leading up to his wife's capture.

"Now this is the way I want you to go about locating her..."

"If it's all the same t' you, I can handle that okay."

Up came one ungloved hand. "I'm speaking now. You'll have every opportunity to respond. After all, I'm on top of this miserable affair, you... you're just coming on board. I've done a great deal of thinking, analyzing the few known facts." He brought out a piece of paper, unfolding it, laying it on the bed for Raider's scrutiny. It was a crudely drawn map. It showed Collardsville in the center. To the left and slightly above the town was an X indicating where Adrienne Dubois had been last seen. Three inches above it were a series of horizontal Xs.

"Adrienne's abductors fled north to one of these seven spots."

"Who says?"

"My dear chap, isn't it obvious? They were Oglala Sioux, that's been established beyond question. It stands to reason, therefore, that they would head back into their own territory."

"Maybe, maybe not."

"I've studied the situation in depth. The Cheyenne are to the west here, the Pawnee to the east, the Arapaho are south. Indians do tend to stick to their own territory."

"Maybe, maybe not. Depends."

Dubois folded his map and handed it to Raider, setting it in his hand and folding his fingers over it.

"Keep this, it should help you immeasureably."

Raider handed it back. "You keep it, I don't need it. I know that neck o' the woods like your pointin' finger knows your nose."

"Raider, I have the distinct impression that we're getting off on the wrong foot here. Let's get one thing clear at the outset. I'm hiring the Pinkerton Agency to find my wife. Chief Pinkerton has assigned you to the task. You are in my employ. You will do as I tell you. I'm not an unreasonable man; actually, I'm the soul of cooperation, but I'm well ahead of you on this and it would be utter folly on your part not to listen to what I have to say and weigh and follow my suggestions."

As he spoke his features took on a hardness, a haughty, authoritative cast. He was not talking *to* Raider, but rather *down* to him. He could not hide his distaste for him any more than he could for their immediate surroundings. Raider had encountered his type before, many times. He was an insufferable prig, a snob, an elitist who thought nothing of demeaning and insulting those he considered his social inferiors. His hands showed that he'd never done a day's hard labor in his life; the softness around his mouth, his delicacy of manner confirmed it. He was a sheltered, pampered, spoiled rich boy and just being in the same room with someone like Raider stretched his tolerance to the snapping point.

Raider didn't like him. The more Dubois talked, the more he stared sourly at Raider as he did so, the deeper the Pinkerton's dislike became. Again and again he was on the verge of interrupting, telling him to shut his mouth, to get out and let him go back to sleep.

But he could not. There was the woman, his wife Adrienne. She was in deep trouble; he'd been assigned to rescue her, he pitied her and very much wanted to. And she wasn't to blame for her bigmouthed snob of a husband. As all these considerations sped through Raider's mind, Dubois abruptly changed his tune.

"I'm a desperate man, Raider. I adore her, worship her. Every minute we're apart is pure agony; knowing, imagining the worst. These hideous pictures that I can't shake from my mind. I'm at my wit's end, I'm going to crack, I know I am. You must get her back. I implore you!"

"I'll do my best."

Again, abrupt change. Face, tone of voice, everything that conveyed the mood of the man.

"You'll get her back. Your chief tells me you're his best man; in dealing with savages you are. Shrewd, knowledgeable, experienced. I'm counting on you. You're all I have." Up came his forefinger, waggling threateningly. "If you fail, if you bungle this, you'll wish you'd never set eyes on me."

"Shit, I already do."

Dubois glared, tightening his hands into fists till his knuckles turned pure white, and he trembled. But he quickly regained control of himself.

"We don't have to be Damon and Pythias to work together in this thing. All I ask is that you follow orders."

"All I ask is that you find yourself another boy."

"See here!"

"You know something, Mister? I feel real sorry for your missus. Not just 'cause the Oglalas got her, but also 'cause she's stuck with you. You purely rub me the wrong friggin' way. I don't like you."

Dubois listened, seething. Then the suggestion of a smile stretched his tightly clamped lips.

"Well there you are; we do have one thing in common. Enough bantering and sniping. When will you be fit to board the train?"

"Day after tomorrow. *If* I do."

"What will you be doing in the meantime?"

"Mendin'. Chrissakes, I'm wounded in two places, remember."

"I know, I know, it's only that time is so devilishly precious. Every hour, every minute, counts."

"They won't hurt 'er."

He tried to catch the words before they got out, but failed to. It was a stupid thing to say. It opened a can of beans every one of which promised to be rotten. Up came Dubois's head, his eyes widening, and swiftly filling with hope.

"They won't?"

"Prob'ly won't."

"What the devil are you saying? Aren't you familiar with the Oatman case?"

Raider sighed inwardly and silently upbraided himself for his carelessness. Who didn't know about the Oatman case? Olive Oatman was only thirteen when her family's California-bound wagon was attacked by Yavapai Indians in a desolate part of the Gila River Valley. Everyone was killed in minutes except Olive and her sister Mary Ann, aged seven, who were carried off to serve as slave laborers. A year later the Yavapais sold them to some Mojaves, who walked the girls north to their settlement on the Colorado River. Here life improved to some extent. The girls were beaten less often and were allowed to grow corn and melons. Two years after their capture a terrible drought struck and many in the tribe starved to death, including frail little Mary Ann.

But Olive was not alone in the world. Her older brother, Lorenzo, left for dead by the Yavapais at the scene of the massacre, had survived. He made his way to safety. He started what turned out to be a five-year search for his sisters. He came across a Yuma brave who knew of Olive's whereabouts and, when Lorenzo bribed him, arranged for her release. In her Indian garments, her skin burned brown by the sun, Olive Oatman was all but unrecognizable when she reached Fort Yuma. She would not speak but sat with her face buried in her hands. It was nearly six months before she emerged from her daze; in time she toured the lecture circuit and submitted to the gawking of the audiences, and eventually she married. She had always been quiet and reserved, but her great suffering with the Indians sat her distinctly apart from the world.

It was more than suffering that isolated her. Like the Mojaves she lived among, she had been garishly tattooed on her arms, the chin, and along the jawline. For the rest of her life she carried on her beautiful and somber face the evidence of her former bondage.

Fanny Kelly has been abducted by the same Oglalas that held Adrienne Dubois. They turned her over to the Blackfoot Sioux and, after five months, she was exchanged for three horses and a load of food supplies at Fort Sully, in Dakota Territory.

Life among their captors was harsh and cruel for both women, but both asserted that they had never been sexually molested. Whether they had and were reluctant to admit it was the question on everybody's mind.

"I know about all the cases," said Raider. "In damn near every one the woman either got away, was let go, or was exchanged for and come out of it without bein' hurt."

It occurred to him to ask if Adrienne had long hair and if it was one of her outstanding features. Long hair, especially long red or blond hair was highly prized by all Indians. And the fact that it grew on another's head was no obstacle to acquiring it. He didn't ask about Adrienne's hair.

"I pray to God in heaven she'll survive unharmed," said Dubois. "At that, she very well could survive in body, only to have her mind snap from the ordeal, poor darling."

He hauled out a gold watch half the size of a baseball.

"It's after nine-thirty. I must be going. I'll be back in the morning."

"For what?"

"We must talk. We've scarcely scratched the surface."

"I think we done all the scratchin' we need. All I need. Look: I know you're worried. It stands t' reason. I got eyes, I can see it's tearin' you apart, but you gotta understan' one thing. There's really nothin'—I mean zero—you can do t' help. It's all up t' me. I'll head on up t' Collardsville day after t'morrow, get my bearin's, check round. By the way, you never did say how you know it was the Oglalas who grabbed 'er."

"A couple passing through spotted the party at a distance. They described what she was wearing to a tee. Of course by the time they got back to town it was much too late to give chase. Which is why I think you should keep this map with you."

"I really don't need it, Edgar."

"Suit yourself."

"I'm gonna. That's the way I op'rate."

Dubois put on his cloak and hat and retrieved his walking stick.

"I'll be by in the morning."

"You got no reason to. We talk anymore, we'll just be kickin' a dead horse, goin' the same route round the barn. Best thing you can do for yourself is catch the train back t'

Collardsville, go back t' work, keep busy; it'll help keep your mind off things."

"Are you serious?" His lip curled disdainfully. "Have you any concept of the turmoil I'm in, the absolute torture I'm going through?"

"I know."

Dubois tapped his hat, frowned, and started for the door. His hand on the knob, he turned.

"You know. That's interesting. Only how could you?"

With this parting shot, he was gone. Raider stared at the closed door.

"I guess I don't, Mr. High-an'-Mighty."

He went back to bed, setting his mental alarm clock to awaken him early. Get up, get out, and stay out. Let Dubois come looking for him. He'd make it his business to stay out of his sight until he boarded the train the day after tomorrow.

"It's for your sake, Edgar. Next time we come face t' face I just may feel good 'nough t' pop you in the mouth when you start 'busin' and insultin' me."

CHAPTER THREE

Raider changed his mind. He boarded the first train out the next morning. He would travel west to Junction City and there change to the line that would take him north, into Nebraska, to Collardsville. He wasn't in great shape to travel, but figured that he could doze away most of the hours, which could only hasten his recovery.

He sat back in his seat and put his mind on the assignment. Pinkerton was right about one thing, if ever there was one: this was a one-man job. A bit like sticking his hand into a snake's nest, groping around and trying to find the pregnant one and pulling her out. Without being nipped. Not that Adrienne Dubois was any rattler; the pictures Pinkerton and her husband had painted in his mind depicted her as a beauty. How beautiful she'd look after the Indians got through with her he'd rather not dwell on.

The big question was how to go about kidnapping the kidnapped. Then getting her out of the camp without either of them losing their hair or catching an arrow between the shoulderblades. As usual, as he saw it from this distance, he'd be playing it "as she goes," keeping his wits about him, being careful, patient, and above all lucky.

Luck had never been one of his strong suits. Any success in anything that came his way was generally hard won, as had been the case with the recent train robbery. His arm twinged and his ribs stung as he recalled the shootout; Fisk dead on one side, Ormsby dead on the other. Once again he saw the outlaw framed by the car door, his back to Raider. He realized that, under the circumstances, more than one man he knew wouldn't have hesitated to shoot the outlaw in the back, but Raider didn't backshoot.

"Good morning."

He stiffened, swallowed hard, and slowly turned his head, lifting his eyes. Dubois beamed almost sadistically.

"Leaving so soon? Move over."

He sat down next to Raider.

"Jesus Christ, what're you doin' here?"

"What does it look like, old chap? I'm your traveling companion. Oh, don't make a face like that. It doesn't promise to be any more enjoyable for me. In case you're wondering, I was standing in the doorway of the hospital opposite your hotel at seven this morning. I had a hunch you might try to avoid me. I followed you around town, watched you eat breakfast at Roessler's Restaurant—my, you do have a hearty appetite!—followed you to the station, and *voila!* We change at Junction City."

"This is a big train, at least a dozen cars. Can't you find another one?"

"Seriously, Raider..."

"I am serious!"

"Lower your voice, man, and don't you talk to me in such a fashion. Even in jest!"

"I don't wanna sit with you, okay? You're a royal pain in the ass."

"Look, let's be grown up about this thing, shall we? And halfway civilized. In your case, even if it hurts. We're going to be working together, we can at least behave like gentlemen. Is that too much to ask?"

"Who says we're workin' together? Who?"

"I do. I did a lot of thinking after I left you last night. I decided that I should go with you, accompany you into their territory. She's my wife. I have a responsibility as her husband. I owe it to her. I... I'd be less than a man, and unworthy of her respect if I stayed home and let you go it alone."

"Oh horseshit! If you really thought that, you never woulda got your old man to contact Mr. Pinkerton in the first place, Chrissakes. You'd be up there round Hat Creek, up into the Black Hills right now. You sure as hell wouldn'a come runnin' down here."

"You're dead wrong, plowboy."

Raider's eyes threatened to burst from their sockets. His face crimsoned, his hands rose as if threatening to strangle his insulter. He sucked his lungs full and let the breath out slowly and steadily, while Dubois watched in astonishment.

"Don't you never call me that again! You do and I'll break you in half."

"You're still wrong. I love my wife.... Where are you going?"

"T' find another car. First stop is Lawrence. I'll be gettin' off there."

"No."

"Don't worry, I'm not quittin' on ya, just takin' a break from your face. You go up on this train, I'll go up on the next, that way we won't have t' squabble all day an' all night. I'm just not up t' it. Not up t' you, Mister."

Dubois eyed him steadily, unflinchingly for fully a minute. Then his face fell and his shoulders sagged in surrender.

"All right, all right, have it your way."

"Which in this here thing is the only way. The quicker you get that through your head, the better off we'll both be. If I'm goin', I go alone."

"I could be a big help to you. You'd be in complete command, that goes without saying, it's your bailiwick, any man would be a fool if he..."

"I said *no,* goddamnit to hell!"

"Sssssh, people are looking. Very well, only promise me this: if you decide to come back to Collardsville after you've located her—before you make your move; come back for assistance, more ammunition or whatever—promise you'll come to me first. Bring me up to date."

"When I go out I won't be comin' back; not without 'er..."

"Dead or alive; say it."

"You say it. You bore the livin' hell outta me, you know that?"

"I'm not accustomed to being addressed in such a fashion!"

"You bring it on yourself. Now get up an' change seats with me."

"What for?"

"I wanna catch some shuteye, I need t' lean 'gainst the window post. Get up, Chrissakes!"

When Raider wasn't stepping off enroute to get a bite to eat or confining himself to the necessary to make room for the next bite to eat, he either slept or pretended to. Unfortunately this did not discourage his uninvited traveling companion from bending his ear. On and on he prattled about his life, his job, his wealth, his wife, his marriage. He took an unwilling Raider by the hand and led him through his and Adrienne's courtship, his proposal, her acceptance, the wedding, the honeymoon in Chicago. "Can you imagine, the honeymoon suite in the La Salle Hotel. Forty dollars a day. And after that we went on to New York and then to Europe. Starting from Paris, we toured the continent. Two and a half months. It was extraordinary, enchanting. We had the time of our lives. Are you a married man?"

"Hell no. I never been on the chain gang neither."

"Priceless, you do have a bizarre sense of humor. Let me tell you, marriage isn't as bad as you think. Of course it isn't for everybody, but it certainly is for us. You've never seen a more devoted couple. Adrienne worships me. Being up on a pedestal does have its drawbacks, though. One must be in complete command of his emotions at all times; once you've gained their respect in order to keep it you've got to be worthy of it. Nothing impresses a wife more than a firm hand on the tiller. She has to know who's boss. It keeps the relationship in proper balance. And it's even more important if you have children. They should look up to their father as if he were a god. And if their mother doesn't, well, blah, blah, blah, blah . . ."

After what seemed an eternity Collardsville came into

view. Raider felt a little like what Moses must have felt upon entering the promised land at last. To his relief Dubois did not invite him as a guest in his house for the day or so it would take him to prepare for his quest. Raider got the feeling that by now the banker was sick of the sight of him, too.

They got off the train and stood facing each other on the platform. Disembarking passengers and those climbing on milled about. The baggage car ramp was down and crates and boxes were being wheeled on board.

"You'll need a place to stay. Try the Collardsville Hotel. It's just up the street; you can't miss it. It's a trifle seedy, but that wouldn't bother *you*. That is, I'm sure you're used to roughing it."

"Yeah."

"Stop and look in on me at the bank before you ride out."

"Yeah."

"I mean it, Raider, I would think, for a man in my unhappy position, it would be the very least you could do."

"No, the least I could do is bring your wife back alive."

"Do you have a plan?"

"Hell no. First thing I gotta do is talk t' people, see if I can put t'gether some information that might help."

"Such as?"

"What about this man an' wife who reported seeing her being kidnapped?"

"I think their name is Frazier."

"Locals?"

"Not living in town, actually, but somewhere close by. Talk to Sheriff Gatling."

"Like the gun?" Raider dispelled Dubois's blank expression. "Gatling gun. Okay. See you round."

Off he trudged, feeling Dubois's eyes pressing into his back, unfriendly eyes, disdainful, arrogant, and scornful. *Poor bastard*, Raider mused, *to think such a fine, upstanding pillar of the community is forced to put all his hope and faith and trust in a plowboy like me.*

Sheriff Meshach Gatling was constructed along the lines

of Dr. Milner's Nurse Fidler. In addition to his obesity, he was encumbered with a game leg. He looked to Raider as if he hadn't sat a horse in thirty years. He was one of those peace officers everybody came to; he didn't go out after lawbreakers, he didn't get out of his swivel chair. It looked like part of him, part of his body, built around his capacious rump and filled almost to the breaking point with his increased weight over the years. It looked as if it would take two crowbars and a team of sturdy draft horses to pull him of his chair.

"In answer to your question, no, I ain't no kin to Dick Gatling who thought up the gun. He's a Easterner."

"I didn't ask."

"You were gonna, evvybody does. So you're a Pink, eh? Come lookin' for Miz Dubois. I wish ya luck, I do; better you'n me, I say."

He swiveled his chair, took dead aim at the spittoon and let fly. With the toe of his boot he hauled open the bottom drawer of his desk.

"I don't bend too good, they's a bottle o' rye down in that some'eres."

Raider downed a generous swing. And immediately regretted it.

"Goddamn stuff tastes like sheep dip," he muttered.

"You're welcome to you," responded Gatling, leering and tipping up the bottle, downing a good half of what remained.

"These people—the Fraziers—who claimed they saw the woman kidnapped."

"Oh, that they did, all right," said Gatling. "I've knowed Wes Frazier a dozen years, he's upright as the preacher. He don' lie, he don' 'zag'rate. No sirree Bob."

"What exactly did he say him and his missus saw? Did he rec'nize the Injuns? I know he said Oglala Sioux, but there's all diff'rent tribes o' western Sioux. Could they 'a been Tetons? Brulés? Blackfeet? Hunkpapas? Minniconjous, Sans Arcs, Two Kettles? Any idea?"

Gatling's little eyes sparkled with admiration. "Lordy me, you sure do know your Injuns. I didn't know they was so many diff'rent tribes. But how could Wesley tell one from t'other? How would you? I'll be jiggered, I never knowed the Blackfoot was a Sioux..."

"Blackfoot Sioux, not reg'lar Blackfeet. There's little things that tells 'em apart. Like the number o' notches in their feathers, the number o' slices for the throats they cut. There's allus lots more with the branches that are on the warpath day in an' day out: the Brulés, Tetons, an' the like. My hunch is she was grabbed by a huntin' party o' one o' them, not the Hunkpapas, Minniconjous, or Sans Arcs. Which aren't quite as bloodthirsty."

"Sittin' Bull is a Hunkpapa."

"Well, the Minnis and Sans Arcs, anyways. It's just that I'd like t' be certain sure who's got her 'fore I go out lookin'. It could help."

"Wesley said Oglalas, and he knows his Injuns. Lordy me, he's sure 'nough tangled with 'em often 'nough."

"Damn, I was afraid o' that."

"I don't folly you..."

"Oglalas move round more than any o' the others. Never in one place more'n a week or two, 'cept during the winter. I sure can't sit around twiddlin' my thumbs waitin' for the snow. That'd make it easy. They'd head for the Powder River country; they allus do, come heavy weather."

"Seems to me your best bet'd be to head north and ask evvybody you come across if they seed a huntin' party with a white woman."

Raider grunted. He picked up the empty bottle and eyed it yearningly, then set it on the desk.

"Got no more," said Gatling. "Sorry."

"That's okay. I'm feelin' a little sickish, anyways. Rye whiskey does that t' me. I got stiffer'n a plank on it down t' Cartwood, got sick as a dog."

"So why you drink it?"

Raider sat up straight, eyeing him as if he couldn't believe he'd asked such a question.

"I *like* it, that's why. As t' anybody seein' a huntin' party with a white woman, that'd be the longest long shot there ever was. Injuns is smarter'n that. That party come within a desert mile of a white settlement they'll wrap her up so you wouldn't rec'nize her as white if you passed her by and touched elbows."

"Like I said afore, I wish you luck. I sure don' envy you the job."

"Me, neither."

Gatling raised his beady eyes to look at the door behind Raider, to make sure, the Pinkerton gathered, that nobody was about to walk in. The sheriff lowered his huge head and his voice in a manner that suggested a conspiracy was afoot.

"Tell me somethin' off'n the record, whadja think o' his nibs?"

"Dubois?"

"King Edgar the Great. 'Swhat folks aroun' here call him behind his back. You ever meet anybody so high and mighty in all your born days? Ain't he somethin'?"

"He's a asshole. I had to ride the train with 'im all the way up from Cartwood. I couldn' even change my friggin' seat t' get away; he'd just change along with me. I pretended I was sleepin' an' didn't hear. He never stopped talkin', spoutin' off, braggin', lordin' it over me how rich he is, how important, how much his wife adores him."

"Ha, shit, too! It's the other way round. Adrienne Dubois is one fine figger of a woman. Got a shape on her that'll make you swally and tingle down in your jewels. And the face of a angel. Feisty, too. Knows 'er mind and ain't afeerd to speak it. Why in hell a woman like that ever hooked up with the likes o' him, practically throwed herself at him, folks say, is more'n I can savvy. Women sure is strange critters."

"He's rich, that's why. Nothin' strange 'bout that."

"I guess.... What I really don' savvy is that she seems downright happy bein' married to him. And she's not stupid; been to finishin' school and evvythin'. Bright as a new penny. And faithful to him, loves him, respects him. So evvybody claims. Lordy me, it does baffle."

"Maybe she's just, you know, what they call clois...

clois . . . wrapped up in a coccoon, cut off from worldliness an' people an' things, a little girl in the body of a woman. Along he comes, she's green as grass, he dazzles her t' beat the band, an' she falls like a barn in a blow. Could be he was the first man she ever even kissed."

"Maybe. Only that man is sure 'nough a first class horse's ass. Evvybody says it's his daddy spoiled him rotten." Gatling shook his great head and frowned disapprovingly. "Fathers'll do that, 'specially the rich ones. Lordy me, my daddy used t' beat me with a willow switch six times a week."

"My step-paw used a short pine plank."

"Let me tell you what Edgar pulled on me back las' fall. I was in the bank jus' standin' there ajawin' with Willis Blakely, the druggist, when another fella calls to me from the doorway. I had my back to it. I turned round real fast, lost my footin' . . . You know how you do when you turn too fast. Tried to catch myself to keep from fallin', Edgar was walkin' crossways, I come down on his foot. Like to squash it flat. Well, you shoulda heard the to-do he put up. You'da thought he'd been run over by a Santa Gertrudis bull. I didn't hurt him, couldn't have, I mean I slipped my foot right off soon's I made contact. Mister, he called me every name in the book and a few I ain't never heard before. Not cursin'; just insults: clumsy oaf, awkward tub o' lard, stupid, ignorant, moronic, bungling. I stood there with my face hangin' outta my collar, feelin' my cheeks gettin' redder by the minute, evvybody standin' starin' at me. Then the son of a b . . . 'scuse my French, runs outta breath and walks away."

"I could see from the way he walked he wasn't hurt or nothin'. No limp, no gimp. It wasn't till after, I found out from one o' the tellers that he had on his newest pair o' Eyetalian soft leather shoes, imported from It'ly. Cost him a fortune and he was mortal afeerd I'd scratched 'em or scuffed 'em. Left me standin' there, walked straight into his office, called in Hector, the office boy, and ordered him to get out the polish and repair the damage."

"Sure sounds like him."

Gatling nodded. "Mind tellin' me if you got any kinda plan worked up for rescuin' her?"

I gotta find her first. I thought about it, o' course. I plan t' pack one saddlebag with grub an' a couple boxes o' forty-fives and the other with junk jewelry. Get me a drummer's suit o' clothes, not as loud as some wear, but not these duds. Pack my Peacemaker an' ammunition in with my grub."

"Ain't that a bit chancy? I mean, shouldn't you be wearin' it where you can get at it in a hurry?"

"No. If I blunder into 'em, or if they spot me afore I do them, it's better for me it's stashed in the bag. For three reasons. Salesmen don't usually wear their irons. Second, I'll strike 'em as bein' a good deal more peaceful, less of a threat, if I'm bare-belt. Third, they'll think I'm a brave man to be ridin' round unarmed."

"Brave or loco."

Gatling pulled open the drawer above the one from which he'd taken the bottle. He got out a palm-sized four-barrel Sharps derringer with a yellowed ivory grip. It was loaded by sliding the barrel unit forward. It was a woman's weapon; women and gamblers resorted to them.

"I took it off a card sharper passin' through here. You could strap it round your leg just 'bove your boot top like a Barns one-ball."

"I could at that."

"Lil' handful o' life insurance, you might say. Isn't worth a dang at more'n ten feet or so, but close up it can kill."

He got out the holster and slender belt that tied double around a man's leg. And a nearly full box of smokeless .22 caliber shorts.

"I'm obliged t' you, Sheriff."

"Meshach—you know, Shadrach, Meshach, an' Abednego. Don't mention it, I only wish I could come along and give you a hand." He stopped short and scowled. "No, I don't. What am I sayin'? I wouldn' trade places with you for a hatfulla gold."

Raider grunted and thought he wouldn't either if he were in the fat man's skin.

"Anything else you need? I got some collection in the back room, more danged artill'ry than you can shake a stick at. You gonna pack a rifle?"

"No. The last thing I want is t' get into a tussle with 'em. What I'd purely prefer is t' deal for her, trade my trinkets, mirrors an' suchlike for her an' walk outta camp slow an' easy, leavin' 'em smilin'."

"You gotta hope."

"I know."

"Maybe you oughta pack a prayer book."

"Tell you one thing I could use, you happen t' have a pair o' field glasses?"

"No, but I do got the nex' bes' thing. Opera glasses."

He excused himself and tried to get out of his chair, but quickly gave up the effort.

"Look in the back on the second shelf over the safe."

Raider found a pair of opera glasses covered in black moroccan leather, with an enameled frame and draws, and clear, unscratched lenses. The glasses looked virtually brand new.

"I conf'scated 'em from the same pilgrim I got the Sharps off'n," explained Gatling. "In lieu o' money he didn' have to pay his fine. Keep 'em. Hope they come in handy. They're not as good as field glasses by a long shot, but better'an the naked eyeball. Give a look 'cross the street."

He was right, the magnification wasn't nearly as powerful as the army-issue field glasses Raider had occasionally resorted to in the past, but they were a good deal better than the unmagnified eye. And they were small and would fit in the breast pocket of his shirt.

Raider thanked him for everything. Gatling wished him luck, accompanying his good words with a deeply worried expression, which served to test what meager confidence Raider had managed to engender in his mission to this point. As Raider was going out the door, Gatling got out his mouth organ and sent him away with "I'll be Glad When You're Dead, You Rascal, You."

Not an intentional needle on his benefactor's part, Raider assured himself, but something less than encouraging.

CHAPTER FOUR

Near the White River Badlands in the southwest corner of Dakota Territory the land tilts upward suddenly, a mountain complex erupting from the plains. Its towers and pinnacles reach well over 7,000 feet at Harney Peak. Grandly revealed as well by the upheaval sixty million years before, are volcanic materials that have welled up into other rock along the northern end of the Black Hills uplift. The original sedimentary layers overlying the region were peeled away by erosion, except for the remnants flanking the Black Hills uplift. They lie steeply tilted, as if they had slid off the table of heaven, there on the eastern side of the Red Valley. The valley is red because it is cut into the reddish Spearfish shales, deposited 180 million years ago, and now bent up and exposed to the forces of erosion. The ridge, known as the hogback, forms an almost continuous rim around the Black Hills.

Between this rim and the central core lies a plateau of Paleozoic limestones in which abundant fractures permit the percolation of ground water. Through combination with gases from the surface, the water has become slightly acid and over many years has dissolved out numerous passageways. Best known of these are Wind Cave and Jewel Cave. Wind Cave is so named because of the rush of wind in and out of the natural entrance. Its trails descend more than 300 feet below the surface. Jewel Cave, a few miles northwest of Wind Cave, is named for its crystals of calcite, a form of calcium carbonate which occurs in sharp-pointed rhombic crystals known as dogtooth spar.

Above the caverns the limestone plateau supports an open forest of ponderosa pine. Mountain mahogany grows there, too, and mariposa lily, mallow, lupine, and fireweed. Deer, elk, and bighorn sheep wander the trails of the Black Hills. Buffalo, prairie dog, badger, and meadowlark populate the open meadows. Raccoons, chickadees, woodpeckers, grouse, and other life forms abound.

The Indian. The Oglala Sioux. One hunting party in particular has come to the Black Hills. Sixteen well-armed hunters led by He-Dog, the best friend of the legendary Crazy Horse, whose blue eyes and light hair make him stand out among his people like a flag in a meadow, adding polish to his reputation among his paleface enemies, many of whom consider him the best cavalry tactician on the continent.

He-Dog wears his straight, black hair down below his broad shoulders unbraided, unbound. His face is relatively thin, though the shape of his jaw, his high cheekbones, mouth, nose, and eyes attest to his blood. He is tall for a Sioux, as tall as a northern Cheyenne, the tallest of the tribes. He disdains the white man's firearms, preferring to hunt with a bow and arrows. He can drive an arrow halfway up its shaft into a moving buffalo's shoulder from 150 feet. He can kill a man at half again that distance. He is younger than Crazy Horse, who himself is barely thirty. He-Dog is fearless in battle, dedicated to the liquidation of the white intruders, and prepared to give his life to the cause. He has only one weakness, if such it can be termed; a quality of humanity which surfaced, quite surprisingly, only a few hours earlier.

He has fallen in love with a white captive.

No Indian displays his affection as white men do. He would never be so childishly and absurdly conspicuous. At all times in front of others he maintains his reserve. A woman's place in the tribal social scheme of things is equal to that of a child or a dog. There is no ostentatious display of affection or kindliness or even interest. No pecks on the cheek, no hand holding; none of the outward signs that betray love's linkage. But in spite of his Spartan reserve it is impossible for He-Dog to hide his feelings when he turns his eyes on his new love. Impossible to control his expression.

The hunting party had headed north to the Black Hills with their prisoner. Their people waited for their return in a series of caves situated between Wind Cave and Jewel Cave. The hunters returned, carrying buffalo and deer meat and some elk, straining the backs of their ponies with the bounty from their hunt.

Crazy Horse greeted He-Dog, who upon arriving, gave his beautiful white captive into the keeping of the squaws, taking pains to warn them that she was not to be harmed, teased, or insulted in any way, driving his knife into the ground in front of a cave and leaving it there as a warning to Black Buffalo Woman, Crazy Horse's wife and titular head of the women.

He-Dog and Crazy Horse sat in privacy on a ledge overlooking the encampment. Below them, the meat that had been brought back was being distributed and tended to by the recipients. A fair wind blew up from the south, rustling the majestic pines close by, the sun blazed in the blue sky above the two men. He-Dog related the events of the four-week hunt, but his listener had heard it all before too many times to be interested. What interested him keenly was obvious.

"We found her picking berries about five minutes at a gallop from the town. Where she was picking she could see it."

"Foolish woman. If Black Buffalo Woman were so careless, so stupid, I would send her back to her husband," rejoined Crazy Horse, his tone intentionally caustic.

He-Dog grinned. "The berries there were very fat and juicy. She is beautiful."

Crazy Horse grunted, unimpressed. "Did any of them see you take her?"

"No one."

"What will you do with her?"

"I have made her my wife."

Crazy Horse's left eyebrow ascended his forehead like a caterpillar rearing, then he grimaced, tilted his head back and forth, and shook it.

"I would not lie with a white woman. Not with my knife within reach of her hand. And they make nothing but trouble with the squaws. They cannot take a beating like a squaw. Remember Real Woman?"

"I remember."

"Then you remember what she did to Jumping Bear. The Blackfeet planned to use her as a ruse to get into Fort Sully and overwhelm the blue soldiers. Jumping Bear saved her life and she repaid him by playing on his feelings, charming him, talking him into secretly carrying a letter to Fort Sully, warning the garrison of the attack. He was disgraced and she was the cause. No one has seen him for two years."

"I am not Jumping Bear."

"You are a man, and she will work on you. You'll see."

"Are you telling me to send her away?"

"No, only to be careful with her." He paused and studied his friend's face, his eyes. "She is in your heart, I can see it."

"So . . ."

"You will come to regret capturing her. You say no one saw you take her?"

"No one."

"Her man will be looking for her. It could bring trouble to us that none of us need."

"It won't."

Again Crazy Horse studied him. Only this time his fixed expression dissolved into a smile. He clapped He-Dog on the shoulder.

"My friend, sometimes I think we should call you Crazy Dog, the things you do. It is your affair, I won't interfere. Only talk to the shaman, he can advise you better than I can."

He-Dog nodded, but only to end the discussion. In his

heart he had no intention of discussing it with anyone. The woman was his. He had already named her Kolata, White Deer. She was his wife now and forever. And if any disapproved, let them; he would ignore them. If anyone harmed her, even Crazy Horse, he would kill him.

CHAPTER FIVE

Raider pushed his frisky little mustang at a steady pace along the dusty road toward distant Coal Creek. The terrain was rugged but not nearly as rough as the limestone plateau the Black Hills sat on up ahead, beyond the Cheyenne River. Raider recalled the last time he visited the Black Hills. He and Doc Weatherbee had chased a bunch of outlaws across the Wyoming border and gotten into a shootout about two miles west of Jewel Cave. It was five against two and had lasted two days and almost two full nights before Raider sneaked up on their fire, and got the drop on them. He and Doc had trussed them up and were preparing to leave when a visitor arrived uninvited: a grizzly with teeth and claws the size of hunting knives and a temper as foul as that of any beast he'd ever encountered. Only Raider's quick shooting had saved their lives. It was a close thing; he'd never seen Doc's cheeks so ashen and his own fear had soaked him with sweat.

He made a mental note to be on the lookout for Mr. Grizzly. Stay out of caves, walk a wide circle around every spot he chose to settle for the night on, and look for signs of bear presence in the area.

He felt uncomfortable in his new duds; not that they didn't fit him, they were just too formal to suit his taste. His taste ran to denims, flannel shirts and boots. Long ago he'd decided that dressing up in suits had been invented by a woman.

"Speakin' o' women, horse, I wonder how the little lady is doin'. I wonder if she's still breathin'."

He unconsciously crossed his fingers and conjured up a

vision of Adrienne based on the descriptions given him by her husband and Meshach Gatling. Then he changed his thoughts to Edgar.

"It sure is good to get away from that sonovagun. Whatta prize."

Riding on between occasional dense groves of pine, he reached the border, identified by a sign that, from the look of it, must have been put up less than a week ago. He pulled up and dismounted. The sun was broiling, and he was sweating furiously as was the horse. He gave her some water from his hat, and downed a couple of swigs himself.

He looked back the way he'd come and could see dust rising into the sun.

"Son of a bitch, I don't believe it!"

Quickly he got the horse off the road and into the trees. He stood holding the reins and waited. Presently the sound of galloping reached his ears and moments later a lone man rode by astride a magnificent bay stallion with silver harness fittings. Raider knew who it would be even before the sound of the horse's hooves arrived. He mounted and rode after him, but not at a gallop, opting instead to let the distance separating them lengthen appreciably, until he reckoned it to be about a mile. There were few straight stretches and it was not until he came to one that he was able to ascertain the distance between them.

He kept back, deciding that rather than catching up with Dubois and confronting him, he'd be smarter to let him run until he stopped to rest and water, then circle around and surprise him from the front. But the banker gave no indication of stopping; from the way he was riding, it appeared that he thought he'd lost his quarry and began spurring his horse to catch up. Within an hour the horse tired and quit on him. Instead of losing his temper, Dubois uncharacteristically recognized that it was his fault for pushing him too hard, got down, and watered and rested the beast.

Raider, meanwhile, circled wide out of sight, dismounted, and ran back, gun in hand. Dubois reacted in surprise when Raider appeared, then broke into a broad smile.

"My word, I thought I'd lost you."

"What're you doin' here, Edgar?"

"That's a stupid question."

"It is, but not as stupid as you are. Get on your horse, turn around, an' beat it. I mean pronto. I got work t' do an' I don't need you taggin' along behind, gettin' in my way."

He fired into the ground at Dubois's feet. His horse started, whinnying plaintively.

"Careful, you nincompoop."

"Mount up!"

"Not a chance. I've come this far, I'm certainly not turning around and going back. Besides, who are you to give me orders? You're working for me, remember?"

Raider said nothing. He holstered his gun, took four steps forward, stopped, brought his right hand up from well below his hip, and hammered him full in the jaw. Crumpling him. Then he stripped off Dubois's belt and bound his wrists securely behind his back. He was still unconscious when Raider led his horse back to where he'd left his own, mounted the mare, and rode off, leading the stallion, resolving to run it a mile at least before he released it. Man would find beast or vice-versa eventually.

"That's the last time you're ever gonna follow me, Edgar old chap."

He flexed his right hand and studied the knuckles. Boy, it felt good belting him, so gratifying, so satisfying. So deserved and such a long time coming.

Picking up Hat Creek and following its west bank north, he came within sight of the Cheyenne River, what the merciless sun had left of it. Summer heat had reduced Hat Creek to a trickle and the river to the creek's normal size. As Raider rode, he considered what the Indians were likely to have done. They were a hunting party finishing up the hunt and would be heading home. The Sioux held the Black Hills sacred, the Oglala especially. Where better to bed down, at least until the hunters returned? Which raised a question. How many hunting parties had been sent out? Certainly more than one. Was this one the last to report in?

If so, by the time he found where they'd gone they could very well have left. Still, he'd be damned if he'd conjure up more problems than he had already. A man's hands can get just so full before things begin spilling over the sides.

The Black Hills—*Paha Sapa* in Sioux—that's where they'd taken Adrienne Dubois.

"Has to be..."

They were home to the Oglala. Honeycombed with natural caves, they were homes that were easily defended and just as easily abandoned; homes that the other tribes stayed away from, knowing the Siouan warlike propensity, Crazy Horse's, Red Cloud's, all the chiefs'. All and a host of others would probably all be waiting for him in the Black Hills. Raider sighed.

"Life don't get any easier, horse. Seems like it should, but it never does for fair."

Above all else, his first, his only priority would be to avoid bloodshed. For the woman's sake as well as for his own. He was dressed for his role and his left saddlebag was fat with junk jewelry. He'd be cool and patient in his dealings. He'd sell like he'd never sold before, convince them that she was worthless; worse than that, she was a bona fide threat. He would tell them that the army at Camp Collins and Gordon Stockade had both been alerted and would be coming to call, no doubt with reinforcements from Camp Collier. The lady was the niece of the governor of Nebraska. Her husband, the governor, her parents, and everyone else in the family were up in arms.

"If you so much as harm a hair o' her head, I guarantee you a thousan' braves'll die. Is she worth one brave?"

He'd be parlaying with Crazy Horse or one of the lesser chiefs. Would they buy what he told them? Would they buy any part of it? Not Crazy Horse, he was as sharp as a steel blade. Still, it depended to some extent on who had grabbed her, whether he was a friend of Crazy Horse's or a foe. If the latter, he'd likely jump at the chance to bust his pride and deprive him of his prize.

Raider wished for about the fiftieth time that he had more to go on, something other than his instincts. One thing worried him mightily: Adrienne Dubois's beauty. If she had been a dog-faced hag like most of the women he knew, whoever'd grabbed her would have little use for her beyond pushing her off on the squaws to share their labor and abuse. But a good-looking woman could be passed from bed to bed like a bottle making the rounds of a campfire.

"She could be fucked t' death afore I get within ten miles o' her, poor soul."

He pictured himself bringing the bad news home to Edgar. Tragic news, the absolute worst, and after knocking him cold and leaving him to wrestle with his belt, unable to squirm free for four or five hours.

"For sure, life don't get any easier..."

CHAPTER SIX

Raider slept that night in his sugan on a bed of pine needles, taking pains before he retired to inspect the area for signs of bear. He was awakened by a loud clanging, a stick banging a frying pan in the hands of a grizzled old sage rat attired in rags, not a tooth in his smile, only half a boot on one foot, and a stink about him that set Raider's eyes watering ten seconds after he opened them.

"Up and at 'em, pilgrim!" croaked his awakener. "Bacon's 'bout to go into the pan, coffee's burblin', biscuits warmin'."

"Who the hell are you? Whatta you mean wakin' a man outta his sound sleep! What the hell time is it, it's still dark out, Chrissakes!"

"Is like hell. Sweet Christopher, you wake up this orn'ry every mornin'? 'Smatter, you got bile in your blood?"

"Go away, lemme sleep."

Raider rolled over. The old man leaned down and whacked the pan loudly six inches from his ear. Raider jumped up, furious.

"You crazy old sonovabitch! Beat it! Get outta here!"

"Calm down, just funnin' with you. Ain'cha got no sense o' humor? Jesus, what a grouch. Let's go, climb outta that raggedy old sugan and lend a hand here. You see to the Java, I'll take care o' the biscuits and bacon. What's your name, Grouchy?"

"Sittin' Bull. What d' you care? None o' your bus'ness. Phew, man do you ever stink! You smell like a barrel fulla farts. Don't you ever wash?"

"Never. Never will. Bathin's bad for you, it'll ruin your constitution. Soap closes up your pores, makes you sweat inside 'steada outside, makes you sick, and in time can kill you, don't you know that? No sir, me an' soap an' water ain't even on noddin' terms. Don't drink water, neither, it's just as bad for you. Seventy-one years young an' never ailed a day in my life. Never been to bed for sick, never had a head cold, the ague, headache..."

"All right, all right, who cares."

"What's your name, Sittin' Bull?"

"Raider."

He wiped his hand on his filthy pants and proferred it. "Mine's Amory Wiggins. Pleased t' meetcha."

Raider hesitated before grasping the outstretched hand. It was filthy as was the wrist attached to it. He averted his head to avoid the stink and, groping for the hand, shook it.

"That's better," said Amory. "Let's eat."

The bacon was delicious as were the biscuits. The coffee was first rate, the best Raider had tasted in months.

"Where'd you get these biscuits?" he asked.

Amory raised his palms. "Made 'em with these two hands."

Raider stifled a groan. Nevertheless, he thought, they were delicious. He could eat ten.

"Where you comin' from, ol' man?"

"Amory, young whippersnapper. Up by Hell Canyon Creek. Headin' back down to Collardsville to get me supplies, vittles, a new pick. Looky over there, that's my mule Eleanor and my horse Harold. Go on over and interduce yourself, why don'cha?"

"No thanks, they look like they stink bad as you do. And man alive, do you ever stink!"

"I don't smell nothin'."

"I don't wonder. Your smeller's prob'ly busted permanent. Ruin't from overwork. Hell, you couldn't smell a polecat if it crawled up your nose."

"Hee hee hee..."

The jibe was merely tossed off, a wise remark, nothing more, but Amory burst into a gale of laughter, too long and too loud. He slapped one knee, then the other, then slapped Raider in the upper arm in friendly fashion and roared. Raider howled in pain and jumped up, swinging his arm and holding it gently fist high.

"What in tarnation . . . ?" began Amory, sobering.

"I had a slug taken outta there a few days back. It was in 'bout seven inches, left a hole you could hide a stack o' poker chips in."

"Sorry. . ."

"Jesus, it hurts, you prob'ly busted the stitches. Whyn'cha keep your hands to yourself, Chrissakes!"

Examination of the wound confirmed that the stitches were intact. Again Amory apologized. The pain receded, Raider recovered, and turned the conversation to the subject he most wanted to discuss.

"You see any Injuns on the way down? A huntin' party?"

"Half a dozen. Any bunch in partic'lar?"

Raider related the story in brief. Amory listened, frowning sympathetically.

"Poor woman. I sure wouldn't wanna be in her place. I didn't see her. Course I weren't that close to them I did see. They're all startin' t' stir up."

"The Oglalas?"

"All the Sioux, but the Oglalas 'specially. Them up in the Black Hills."

"How come?"

"Ain't you heard? Lone-hand prospectors is findin' gold. They's talk it's all over. From Spearfish clear down to Lame Johnny Creek."

"Talk. Man can fill his hat with gold talk."

"I b'lieve it. I'm goin' down t' stock up on supplies an' come back an' find me my share."

"So somebody found some gold. That don't mean there's a load of it, even 'nough t' bother with. A man can dig till he dies an' never find any. You should know. There's lots have."

"You'd sure never make a prospector."

"Why in hell would I wanna be one?"

"You gotta have faith."

"You gotta be stupid."

"There's already forty or fifty of us up there pokin' round."

"Yeah, well you better be careful. That's Injun land by treaty. Eighteen sixty-seven or so a treaty was signed at Fort Laramie, pledgin' the Sioux forty-odd thousan' square miles in the Black Hills. The whole of 'em. Gover'ment gave 'em clothin', rations, and one cow per family. I remember."

Amory leered. "The Lord giveth, the Lord taketh away."

"Well I sure hope the lid don't jump off while I'm up there doin' what I have to," said Raider.

"It won't for a while," said Amory in an encouraging tone.

"I dunno, I figger all I need is a week, maybe only five days, t' find the ones that took her. And her."

"I wouldn' worry about that, my frien'."

"Whatta ya mean?"

"I mean you likely don't stand a chance o' finding them, but . . ." He paused and leered. "They cain't help but find you."

Raider grunted. Truer words were never spoken, he thought ruefully.

CHAPTER SEVEN

Edgar Dubois gingerly repositioned the leather brace supporting his broken jaw. It resembled the protective helmet a prize fighter wears when working out with his sparring partners. It was homely, absurd looking, and uncomfortable, but it served its purpose. Raider's fist had given him a serious fracture and his doctor had prescribed the protective device, ordering Edgar to wear it for a minimum of ten days.

It may have served its purpose, but it also served to advertise his defeat at the hands of his attacker to all and sundry. At the moment, the loser was seated at his desk in his private office at the bank, appending his signature to a letter he'd just finished. Swirling his pen away from the final S in his name, he blew on the ink. Eyeing his door, making certain it was shut, he then read the letter aloud.

Dear Chief Pinkerton,

I will begin by saying this is probably the most difficult letter I have ever written. You, sir, came to my rescue when Mrs. Dubois was apprehended by the savages. A nobler and more timely gesture I cannot conceive of. I reveled in the relief that filled my breast when the vaunted, the estimable Pinkerton National Detective Agency agreed to go to work on my behalf. You assigned Operative Raider to the case. I took it upon myself to call upon Mr. Raider in his hotel room in Cartwood on the evening of the 11th. It grieves me to say that I found him dead drunk, unable to converse coherently, and determinedly uncooperative. I repeat, determinedly. He did me the courtesy of hearing me out, but from that point on refused to listen to my suggestions. He's the professional and I'm only the injured party to be sure, but it seems to me he could have at least behaved civilly. I have to say he is the most pigheaded individual I have ever met. It is not for me to question your judgment or his credentials, but his methods, his tactics for the job, seem woefully inadequate. Indeed, his ideas for rescuing Adrienne threaten to put her in even greater peril of her life.

I'm a reasonable man, and reasonably intelligent. During my ordeal I have suffered greatly. My helplessness holds me in thrall, but I have had time to give a good deal of thought to the situation. I am convinced that if Raider had permitted me to accompany him in pursuit of Adrienne's captors I could have been of use to him: as a lookout, as man of all work, present and prepared to plead with the savages for her release when we came face to face with them. Whatever they demanded in exchange for her, I would gladly give them. I begged to go along. He refused to let me. In the end he lost his temper (the most vicious temper I have ever seen, which leads me to believe that he's not in full possession of his faculties). He attacked me, broke my jaw in four places, bound me with my own belt while I lay unconscious, and rode off, taking my horse. Had it not been for the fortuitous passing of a Good Samaritan in the person of the Reverend Jonas Tyler, whose church here in Collardsville, Adrienne and I attend, I might have perished out there in the wilds of Dakota Territory.

It is in your own interest as well as Adrienne's and mine that I feel compelled to write this letter. I thought that you should be made aware of his disgraceful conduct throughout this sorry affair. In my opinion he is unfit to be employed by your organization, he does your good name harm, he is an illiterate, obnoxious, irresponsible, disgusting, drunken degenerate, and I live in constant fear that rather than rescue Adrienne, he will be the cause of her demise as well as his own.

I ask you, therefore, to remove him from the case and assign another man in his place. One responsible, intelligent, reasonable, capable. Everything that Raider is not. I am a desperate man; the mere thought that Adrienne's survival depends upon such a disreputable individual, an ignoramus, a bullying rowdy, only intensifies my concern. I implore you, replace him. Immediately.

                  Yours very truly,
                  Edgar Howard Walter Dubois, Esq.

He folded the letter and inserted it in an envelope addressed to Chief Allan Pinkerton. Then he changed his mind. He wouldn't send it as a letter. Better to put it into a telegram. Instead of four weeks it would be there in a day.

Kolata's dress was torn at the shoulder, but she herself was unharmed, suffering not so much as a scratch outwardly, suffering the tortures of hell within. Wisely, she had not put up a struggle when He-Dog seized her, bound her wrists, and sat her behind him on his war pony. She had protested verbally, but for only a short time, speedily recognizing that the situation was hopeless. But as the hunting party headed north fear found her stomach and spread its tentacles throughout her upper body, locking about her thumping heart.

She had heard all the stories about white women captured by Indians, and even allowing for exaggeration, they were all frightening. White captives—women and children—were treated as slaves, and mistreated by the jealous squaws. Every woman in the west knew the story of Olive Oatman; the worst thing that the Mojaves had done to her was to tattoo her face hideously. Other captives suffered the tortures of the damned; many committed suicide to free themselves from a life of abuse, degredation, and abject cruelty.

Arriving at the caves, Adrienne had been turned over the Black Buffalo Woman, Chief Crazy Horse's stolen wife. She was a small thin woman with perpetually sad eyes and a purple scar an inch wide that resembled a rope burn circling her throat. To Adrienne's surprise and relief Black Buffalo Woman treated her with kindliness and sympathy. She could also speak some English, a few halting phrases learned years earlier from a trapper who had befriended her first husband. Black Buffalo Woman, a niece of Red Cloud, had been given in marriage to No Water while Crazy Horse was on the warpath. When he came home and learned of what had transpired in his absence he was despondent, but there was nothing he could do about it. After a while he began to visit the camp of No Water from time to time and was able to see and talk to Black Buffalo Woman. Meanwhile he and He-Dog were made lance bearers and thus leaders of a war party against the Crows with lodges and women accompanying the honor. Crazy Horse continued to see Black Buffalo Woman, and in time she placed her three children in the care of relatives and joined him on the hunt. She was a Lakota and Lakota women were free to come and go as they pleased.

Nevertheless, she was married to an important man in the Bad Faces. This may have impressed Crazy Horse's intelligence, but it had little effect on his heart. He set about solving his problem. Instead of dispatching her husband, or arranging with a trusted friend to do No Water in, he boldly confronted him to arrange the purchase of Black Buffalo Woman. No Water was not interested. They argued. No Water pulled a gun and shot him in the face, leaving a scar that hideously disfigured his cheek and nose. But eventually No water changed his mind about keeping his wife. Perhaps a greedy streak in his nature was touched by Crazy Horse's offer of weapons and horses; perhaps he recognized that Black Buffalo Woman's interest in him had greatly diminished. The fact that she had joined Crazy Horse on the hunt may have persuaded him of this. Perhaps, too, No Water thought twice about the risks to himself in continuing to deny such a powerful warrior the object of his affection. Whatever his reasons, he eventually renounced all claim to Black Buffalo Woman and she married Crazy Horse.

The Bad Faces didn't approve, nor did Crazy Horse's fellow chiefs, but the principals ignored their criticisms. Shortly after No Water gave up his wife, he died in battle.

The captive Adrienne cooked and sewed and did other squaw's chores all day. At night she lay with He-Dog. And life went on. Raider drew closer to the Black Hills. Edgar Dubois went about his work and missed his Adrienne mightily and worried himself sick about her, imagining the worst, his protected fracture gradually healed, and his message flew eastward to its destination.

Late in the afternoon of the second day of his search Raider crossed Horsehead Creek and was starting up into the Black Hills when he passed a prospector's cabin, a neat little pine log structure displaying flowers in twin window boxes under the front windows, a tidy little yard, and the morning wash hanging on a line stretched from the left rear corner to a pole twenty feet from the house.

"Sure is a sight better way o' livin' than old Wiggins's," he thought while passing. Husband and wife must live there, he mused. A woman's touch was in evidence everywhere outside. About 100 yards beyond the house, he turned in his saddle to look back at it. At that moment his horse stumbled. When it regained its footing and resumed its trot, he noted that it was favoring its right foreleg. He reined up, got down, and examined its hoof. A pebble had lodged between shoe and hoof. He freed the stone with his knife, but in doing so, he loosened the shoe. He removed the shoe and walked the horse back to the cabin. The lady of the house had come out to take in her wash. She saw him, smiled, and waved a greeting. Her arms piled high with the laundry, she made her way back to the front door. He stood waiting and when she came up offered to relieve her of her load.

"That's all right, I can manage, thank you."

He had the presence of mind to remove his hat when he introduced himself. She was young, pretty, buxom, with flaming red hair piled up and pinned in the back, and freckles to match. Her name was Frances Hotaling.

"Mrs. Jabez Hotaling."

He showed her the horseshoe. "You wouldn't have a few extra nails lyin' about doin' nothin', wouldja?"

"Oh sure, out back in the tool shed. And a hammer. Can you shoe a horse?"

"In a pinch."

"We can go round back and get 'em, but you're not in any rush, are you? I mean you do have time to stop and visit. I can make us a pot of tea. You like tea?"

He could see that she was starved for companionship. She wore a wedding ring. He wondered if she was a widow. He accepted her invitation and one would have thought he'd agreed to set her on the throne of England from her reaction, so pleased was she.

They sat at the little table in the front room over tea and muffins, freshly baked that morning. He told her of his mission. She appeared impressed with his courage and intrigued by his line of work.

"I've never met a Pinkerton detective before." She laughed brittlely. "Of course I don't get to meet anyone stuck out here. My husband is prospecting for gold up in the hills. He comes home every sundown, goes out bright and early every morning."

"Any luck?"

"Some. Nothing to write home about. He built this place."

"Nice place. He knows his business."

"He's actually a carpenter."

They finished two cups of tea apiece, then she took him around back to the shed and, poking through a number of battered pasteboard boxes, finally turned up a handful of horseshoe nails. She also found him a hammer and a bastard file.

"In case you need it."

He took ten of the nails and returned the rest with his grateful thanks. They went back into the house to finish off the muffins. Ten minutes later he was preparing to leave, was going out the door when she called to him. He turned.

"Promise if you pass this way with her coming back, you'll stop by. Whatever the hour, even the dead of night. She'll need a woman's care..."

"I prom..."

It was as far as he got. A boulder dropped on the back of his head, felling him. The last thing to enter his mind was her shriek.

CHAPTER EIGHT

Raider had once seen the head of a man who had been beaten to death with axe handles. The head had swollen to twice its normal size, turned deep purple, and absorbed the victim's ears and facial features, leaving only the tip of his nose protruding like a button from the loathsome mass of battered flesh that had formerly been his handsome face.

When he awoke to the ringing agony that was his own head all he could think of was the axe handle victim's skull; all he could see was the hideous duplication of it in his suffering mind's eye. His hangover in his hotel room in Cartwood was a mild headache compared to how he felt at the moment he regained consciousness. So severe was the pain, so insideous, he began to gasp, as if to drive it out of his cranial vault with jets of fresh oxygen. It was useless. His head throbbed and ached as if it were going to shatter and even the sight of pretty Mrs. Hotaling's solicitous expression hovering before his eyes and the cool damp cloth being gently applied to the back of his head failed to alleviate it.

As her face came into focus it darkened in annoyance.

"Shame on you Jabez Hotaling, hitting him from behind. You might have killed him!"

"He's all right, he's breathin' isn't he?"

"You've fractured his skull!"

"Don't say that," murmured Raider weakly, "don't even think it, please."

Husband and wife helped him to his feet and into the bedroom, laying him down slowly. He reckoned that he'd only been unconscious a minute or so; God, Fate, Lady

Luck, Mother Nature, somebody awakening him before death could claim him. They lay him back. The instant the back of his head touched the pillow a bolt of pain shot upward from it, blowing his brain to pieces. She turned his head to one side, setting him down on his right cheek. He lay suffering, dying, looking from one to the other, still gasping for all the good it was doing him, and marveling at his host.

Hotaling looked to be about 25, about six foot ten, the crown of his hat rising to within two inches of the ceiling. Raider estimated he weighed upwards of 260 with his boots off. Each shoulder was located better than a foot from his neck, which looked to be a collar size 24. He had his hat on and his shirt off. His arms looked like two railroad ties tightly wrapped with two-inch diameter manilla rope. His chest resembled a potbellied stove. He looked capable of pulling fully grown trees up by the roots. Raider had no idea what he'd hit him with, but either fist looked up to the job. He watched him make the left one. It was as big as a bench vise. He shuttered his aching eyes and sighed inwardly.

"Are you feeling better?" Mrs. Hotaling asked solicitously.

"Mmmmmm."

A little early to ask, he thought. Actually he was feeling rotten, was on the verge of concluding that he'd never feel the same again, that he'd linger in agony for another half hour or so, then pass on.

"Apologize to the man," she snapped, whirling and glaring at the giant beside her.

"Do I have to?"

She pushed him so hard he nearly fell over. She was about two feet shorter than he and little more than a third his weight, but clearly she intimidated him. She was the boss and at the moment she was furious with him.

"I only did it to protect you," Jabez grumbled. "Man's supposed to protect his wife, isn't he?"

"From what, you idiot? He wasn't doing anything. He's been a perfect gentleman. Speak up! Apologize!"

"I'm sorry, I won't do it again."

"Jesus, I hope not," said Raider, just about the first coherent words he was able to articulate loud enough for them to hear.

"We'll let you sleep," she said. "When you wake up, I'll have some hot chicken soup for you. You'll be on your feet in no time."

"I'll shoe your horse for you," said Jabez. "And feed and water her."

They went out—rather she pushed him out and followed—closing the door behind them. Raider slept until sunup the following day. When he woke he felt much better. The pain had reduced itself to a dull ache, and a huge lump that was tender to the touch was forming, but otherwise he was okay. Apart from being famished. He wondered where the Hotalings had spent the night after donating their bed to him. Mrs. Hotaling had slept on the couch in the front room, Jabez in a chair.

Serves him right, reflected Raider when they told him. He ate enough breakfast for two men, including a nine-high stack of hotcakes, washed it and six of her muffins and four soft-boiled eggs down with about a quart of coffee, thanked her and, grudgingly, her husband, and started forth.

By sundown he was well up into the Black Hills. By dark he was within sight of Jewel Cave to his left. He had not seen a single Indian, much less any hunting party. No sign of deserted camps, either, but the Oglalas were somewhere in the hills; he could feel their presence. He prided himself on his sharply honed and most reliable intuition that warned him when a confrontation and possible danger were close. The Indians were here, perhaps watching him at that very moment; they'd meet, and soon.

That night he made his bed under a majestic pine, heaping up needles for his pillow. He decided against building a fire, making do with cold beans and a biscuit for supper. Mrs. Hotaling's mammoth breakfast still stuck fast to his ribs, so he wasn't really hungry. Then too, any fire, even a small, well-hidden one, might catch a roving Indian's sharp eye.

But it wasn't the Indians that worried him, at least not yet. Foremost among his concerns was the threat of a roving grizzly. This was their country even before the Sioux took it. He'd yet to see a bear, even at a distance, but it was likely that he would before he saw Collardsville again. With or without Adrienne Dubois.

Gun in hand he warily searched the area surrounding his bed, looking and listening for bear or any other creature that might approach him as he slept. He found no bear, but did come across the half-eaten carcass of a deer. No Indian would leave his dinner in such condition. He wondered: should he go on for an hour or so? Move further into the hills? Why bother? If anything, that would increase his chances of running into a grizzly. Better to stay where he was and sleep with his cocked Peacemaker in his hand.

His head no longer hurt, nor did either of his wounds. He felt ninety percent sound, and was beginning to look forward to introducing himself to Adrienne Dubois and meeting her captors. He had plenty to offer them in exchange for her. Roughly half his supply of geegaws was mirrors or mirror jewelry, which all Indians treasured. With any luck, he'd be able to make his deal and ride out with her with no difficulty. It had been done, he knew. He could do it.

"Luck..."

He lay under his tree, the branches shielding sight of the stars and moon. He listened to the night sounds and thought about Edgar. He had hit him a good lick, good enough to fell a bull. He pictured him back in Collardsville, back on the job in the bank, sitting at his desk behind his swollen jaw.

"Serves him right for fair..."

He switched his thoughts back to Mrs. Dubois. He would hand over the junk jewelry, the opera glasses, even his gun and ammunition if they demanded them. He'd hang onto the concealed Sharps .22. He would have to have some protection for the ride back.

He slept. And dreamed of Jabez Hotaling, not one but at least a dozen Jabez Hotalings, all giants, all identical, all livid at discovering him with their wives, though he could only manage to conjure up one of her. They surrounded him in the little front room and took turns bashing him over the head, lining up for the purpose, those at the back of the line urging the ones up front to hurry up. They hit him with everything handy, table legs, chairs, stove lids, lid lifters, fists. It was very discouraging. Throughout, Mrs. Hotaling ran about the room like a scared chicken screaming at them to stop. Nobody paid any attention to her.

The sun was already up when he awoke. He knuckled the sleep from his eyes and raised himself on one elbow. He could hear voices. When he finally got his eyes fully open and his brain cleared, he gasped. All around him were Indians, dozens of them, forty, fifty, all armed. Not one paid the slightest attention to him. They had gotten into his saddlebags and had divided up the jewelry. Sunlight stabbed at his eyes from a hundred different mirrors. One brave had found the opera glasses. He was walking around peering through them at the others. Two were arguing heatedly over his Peacemaker. A third stepped between them, snatched it from one and handed it to the other, changed his mind, snatched it back and ran off, the other two in pursuit.

Raider sighed. Two braves behind him lifted him to his feet, his sugar falling to his ankles. In seconds he was surrounded by grinning, gesticulating, jabbering hostiles. One held his wrists behind his back while two others searched his pockets. They found his knife, opening it, holding the point against his throat.

They did not find his Sharps .22 in its little holster fastened to his lower leg.

CHAPTER NINE

The founder and principal of the Pinkerton National Detective Agency personified the slogan he had devised for the organization. Chief Allan Pinkerton *was* "the eye that never sleeps." Dedicated, monomaniacally so, indefatigable, he worked an 80-hour week from early morning to late at night six days running. Not one but two secretaries, working an early and late shift, served him. He spent so much time on the job because so much of it was devoted to close scrutiny of every case the agency's operatives were assigned.

On the wall beside his office door hung a large map of the United States dotted with pins, the majority were red, indicating operatives on assignment. These he was continually shifting as they moved about in the field. At the moment he was moving Raider's red pin from the northwest corner of Nebraska (Collardsville being too tiny to be shown on the map) northward over the border into Dakota Territory.

On the chief's desk lay Edgar Dubois's telegram, containing his less-than-complimentary opinion of Raider and Raider's abilities and the fervent plea that Pinkerton replace him.

Superintendent William Wagner entered in his shirtsleeves, puffing on a cigar.

"You wanted to see me?"

Pinkerton nodded and handed him the telegram. Wagner sped through it, unscrewed his cigar from the corner of his mouth long enough to whistle low in comment, and restored the cigar.

"Great Caesar's ghost.... He's back on the bottle..."

"Foosh, don't be a ninny. When I saw him in that butcher shop that passes for a hospital in Cartwood he'd just had two slugs removed and was in desperate pain. I gather after I left he had an argument with the doctor, walked out, took a hotel room, and proceeded to drink himself insensible to numb his discomfort. I don't approve of his imbibing to excess, but under the circumstances I can understand why."

"Dubois claims he attacked him."

"No doubt he did."

Pinkerton smiled as he said it. In punctuation of an altogether alien, wholly uncharacteristic attack of tolerance on the chief's part.

"Don't look so mystified. You must read between the lines. You haven't had the pleasure of meeting Edgar Dubois. The man is a pampered twit, a snob, and a bore who unquestionably got off on the wrong foot with Raider. Which is putting it mildly. Locked horns with the lad from the outset, foolishly tried to order him about like one of his boot-licking clerks at his bank."

"That wasn't the impression you gave me of Dubois."

"I didn't give you any impression. To me his sort is too distasteful to discuss. Raider wouldn't be on this case—ordinarily I'd give the likes of Edgar Dubois a tip of my hat and the back of my head—were it not for the fact that his father is one of my oldest and dearest friends. Like father like son couldn't be further from the mark than with those two. Harmon is a prince, a man of breeding, education; a loyal, decent, considerate, charming man. His son... spare me going into detail. Still, I could hardly refuse his plea for help just because he rubs me the wrong way."

"He says Raider broke his jaw."

"Pish, tush, and twaddle. Lost his famous temper and punched him, probably. Knowing Raider, unquestionably; knowing Edgar it had to be deserved. And I'm sure he didn't break it, only bruised it a bit and caused it to swell, hurting the lad's pride more than his jawbone." He tittered. "He must have looked quite a sight at the bank the next morning. Read it again, why don't you, mind what he says between the lines. He insisted Raider let him go along on the hunt; he put his foot down, Raider stepped on it. For which I applaud him.

"Don't you see, Will, it's the old story: the plowboy and the plutocrat. Put them in the same room and in sixty seconds they're at each other's throats. When they're as strong minded as Raider and his nibs they are."

A timid knock sounded at the door. Wagner opened it. It was one of the chief's secretaries, who handed the superintendent a second telegram. The chief tore it open and as he read it a smile brightened his usually dour face, lifting the corners of his mouth, setting his eyes twinkling and etching crows-feet at their corners.

Wagner, shorter and stouter than his superior, stood behind one of Pinkerton's shoulders, rising on tiptoe to look over it at the wire.

"He wants four operatives assigned to replace Raider? We don't have four men in the area. We don't have any."

"Hush, Will. Don't get your delicate constitution in an uproar. Its wind, pure hot air, and if you stand aside there, we'll let it blow past us out the window. Mr. Edgar Dubois is out to get Raider."

"He's making it sound pretty hairy," said Wagner worriedly.

"Foosh, it's nothing of the sort. He's too dim-witted and too prejudiced to recognize that Raider's his best hope for her. His only hope. Besides, the die is cast. Raider's well up into the Black Hills by now, possibly already in contact with the woman's abductors."

He placed Edgar's first telegram on top of his second and tore both in quarters, dropping the pieces in his wastebasket.

"Get my secretary in here, would you, like a good chap? I want her to take a telegram. To Mr. Edgar Dubois, Esquire, Collardsville, Nebraska."

His secretary was summoned with pad and pencil. The gist of the telegram he dictated was: "trust Operative Raider; if anyone can rescue your wife, he's the man."

He was tempted to add "whether you like it or him or not," but bridled the urge. He only hoped that his high opinion of and unstinting confidence in Raider would not find its way to his ears. Little did he realize that his rejection of Edgar's plea coupled with high praise for Raider would only intensify the banker's hatred of the Pinkerton.

CHAPTER TEN

It was the task of the Oglala women to prepare the deer and buffalo meat brought in by the hunting parties and a dozen cutting bees were going on simultaneously in the area occupied by Crazy Horse and his followers. Adrienne Dubois worked with one group on a freshly killed buffalo cow, butchering it, soaking her hands to the wrists in blood, unaffected by it, not at all queasy from the sickly-sweet smell and warmth of it, but declining Black Buffalo Woman's offer to sample the raw meat. The squaws showed no such hesitancy. As they cut and slashed they snacked on raw liver; kidneys; the tongue; the eyes, a particular delicacy; and belly fat, ravenously chewing gristle from the snout, marrow from the leg bones, and arguing over the tastiest morsels of all, the hoofs of an unborn calf. An old man sliced the nipples and greedily slurped the warm milk. The belly was slit and the entrails removed, warriors joining the feast, drinking handfuls of warm blood. No one touched the brains. They were a delicacy reserved for the chiefs.

Adrienne did not so much enjoy the grisly chore as she was fascinated by it, by just about everything she'd seen since she'd been captured. Black Buffalo Woman treated her well and was her mentor as well as protector. Adrienne no longer feared for her life, nor did she fear being raped or mutilated. She wisely adopted an attitude of tolerance and patience, no longer looking upon her abduction as an ordeal, but more of an experience, an adventure. Black Buffalo Woman was kind to her, as was He-Dog. None of the women had bothered her yet, apart from one or two squaws who had picked at her clothes and pinched her when she first got there.

She looked over at the ledge where He-Dog sat in consultation with Crazy Horse. So involved were they in discussion, they seemed completely oblivious to the spirited activity and noise all around them. Crazy Horse was the Oglala's youngest warrior chief. And every inch a chief in appearance: blue-eyed, brown-haired, his skin as pale as a white man's. Among his people he stood out like an albino. He sat bareheaded, his light hair shining in the bright sunlight. He-Dog, squatting opposite him, wore a war bonnet with a four-foot row of eagle feathers down the back, each one decorated with bright stripes of beadwork at the base and tipped with a plume fashioned from the hair of a white horse. Each feather was cut, alternating notches for enemies slain and slices for throats cut. On they parlayed, surrounded by the people, smoldering fires before the cave mouths, dogs fighting over bones flung to them by the squaws, naked children, raucous laughter, and horseplay. A squaw was heaping green branches on a fire to drive away the gnats. Others cut and smoked deer meat, buffalo meat, and dark, greasy elk steak.

Adrienne heard shouting. Men and women were pointing southward down through the hills. Another hunting party was returning, their ponies laden with carcasses. She squinted and shielded her eyes from the sun. At the forefront of the party rode two young warriors, between them a man in a black suit; a white man, she guessed from his clothing, although she could not make out his face at that distance. But he was not dressed like a prospector. Her glance drifted from the oncoming party to the two poles standing to the left on a grassy knoll; they were forked and a third pole lay across them. From it the corpse of a prospector hung by the ankles. He had been caught on sacred Sioux land, brought to the camp, hung upside down alive, and stoned and beaten to death by the squaws. He hung like a thick red blanket, the blood released from his body pooling under his head and drying, darkening, no longer reflecting sunlight as it had when it was dripping down during his execution. Two other trespassers' bodies hung in similar fashion. One's puddle had not yet completely dried and still mirrored the sun.

The hunting party came into camp. Their prisoner was a tall, dark-skinned, dark-eyed, rugged looking man. His suit made him look like a preacher, but *he* looked nothing like one, nor like a prospector. More like a hard-working farmer attired in his Sunday best. All activity ceased as the arrivals stopped and dismounted; all eyes were on the white man. He glanced at Adrienne and looked as if he recognized her, although he did not nod or alter his expression. Crazy Horse and He-Dog came down from their ledge.

Raider picked Adrienne out of the crowd from a distance of a hundred yards. They had dressed her in deerskins and she had braided her hair, but there was no mistaking the lightness of her skin. She was even whiter than Crazy Horse, who stood before Raider, looking him up and down without speaking. Then he turned to the braves that had gathered around them and ordered them away. He-Dog, who stood by his side, hesitated and Crazy Horse caught him by the arm. The sub-chief who had led the hunting party that had found Raider finished explaining his presence to Crazy Horse, then left with the others.

"What do you call yourself?" the chief asked in perfect English.

"Weatherbee."

Raider brashly offered his hand, Crazy Horse ignored it. It was no gesture of greeting on Raider's part, but an intentional effort to show that he wasn't frightened, that his hands were clean, his motives pure, that he represented no threat to the tribe. He was not a prospector searching for gold in the Oglala's sacred hills.

"Why do you come into our land?"

"I'm a salesman, His Horse Looking..."

Crazy Horse yielded to the faintest glimmer of a smile. His Horse Looking had been the name he acquired after he had taken part in a raid on an Omaha village when he was thirteen. It was a fact known by no more than a handful of whites.

"Your boys here surprised me, woke me up, ransacked my goods, all my jewelry. I'd 'preciate it if you call 'em all back t'gether and collect it for me. Then I'll just be on my way."

Crazy Horse heard him, but said nothing. He stood with his arms folded, staring at him. He reached out and plucked at Raider's lapel. He then took hold of both of Raider's hands and turned them over to examine the palms.

"Salesman? You are no salesman, not with these hands."

He tilted his head to one side, narrowed his eyes, and studied him further. Then waggled a finger.

"You are a man who lives on a horse, a soldier."

"Not me, no sirree, this look like a un'form t' you?"

"Then a lawman. I will ask you again, what are you doing in these hills?"

Raider reflected a few seconds before answering, his mind racing, careening, deciding that he had no choice but to brazen it out.

"I come for her..."

He pointed at Adrienne, who was standing with a group of squaws about thirty feet from them, looking on. Out of the corner of his eye he could see He-Dog's reaction: his dark eyes flashed in anger and his hand went for his knife, locking about the hilt. Crazy Horse set a hand on his arm to stop him from pulling it.

"I'm U.S. Gover'ment, personal represen'tive of Gov'nor Robert Furnas of Nebraska. That lady there is the gov'nor's niece. It's not for me to criticize nobody, Chief, but your boys couldn't have picked a worse choice to kidnap. Gov'nor Furnas hit the ceiling. An' believe me, the man's got a temper like you wouldn't b'lieve. At this very moment about eight hundred soldiers are 'sembled at Camp Collier, Camp Collins, an' the Gordon Stockade, ready to ride, to surround this camp an' take 'er back. Unharmed, not a scratch. You're a smart man, Chief, you know when t' fight an' when it ain't worth it bettern'n any chief o' the Sioux. And this time it ain't worth it, ain't worth losin' two or three hundred warriors t' the army's guns for her."

"Eight hundred soldiers, you say."

"Maybe a thousan'."

This time Crazy Horse gave in to a smile. It split his face; he even chuckled. His reaction relieved the tension in He-Dog's expression; he, too, smiled. Crazy Horse's smile then gradually gave way to a somber look, a glower.

"You are a liar."

"Like hell, I . . ."

Crazy Horse took one step forward and slapped him with the back of his hand. Raider's hand flew to his cheek; he took a step backward, but someone behind him pushed him forward.

"If the woman is the governor's niece, why did you bring the jewelry with you to bargain for her? Why bargain when you can demand she be released? She is not the niece nor the wife nor the daughter of anyone important; if she was you would not come, the army would. You will not take her, my men have taken you; you do not threaten, demand, or even ask, you are lucky to be still alive. Whether you continue to live or not, I cannot say. Not until I decide what to do with you. Perhaps I should hang you up for the squaws like those gold seekers, who dare to come onto our lands. As you dared. Shall I hang you like them?"

"I'm the personal represen'tive of the gov'nor of Nebraska . . ."

"Be still!"

"All right, all right, no need t' get huffy, I ain't done nothin'. Look, why don'cha make it easy all round, think 'bout what I told you. It's the bald truth. I'm not threatenin', just givin' you a friendly bit o' advice; wash your hands o' this bus'ness, let me go, let me take 'er with me."

"No!" burst He-Dog.

Again Crazy Horse stayed him. He eyed Raider for fully ten seconds, then shook his head.

"All right, all right, think it over. Take all the time you need. Just let me talk to her, okay? Private like."

"No," repeated He-Dog.

"Talk to her," said Crazy Horse. He indicated a nearby cave. "In there, He-Dog's cave."

"I come with you," interposed He-Dog.

Raider eyed Crazy Horse appealingly.

"Let him speak with her alone," said Crazy Horse.

Edgar Dubois was already fed up with his liquid diet, sucking soup and milk and tea through a glass straw, losing weight, fraying his patience, stoking the fire of the disgust and resentment he felt for Raider. Allan Pinkerton's cavalier response to his two telegrams did not help matters. Edgar sat at his desk, rereading Pinkerton's wire, grumbling in his leather protector, and yearning for a juicy steak. The door opened. It was one of his tellers, a small, harassed-looking individual in his late forties, the sort of man born to be dominated by a nagging wife and an unsympathetic world.

"Mr. Dubois, sir, we've finished the totals; we're three hundred eighty-one dollars and fourteen cents short."

"What!"

The word exploded from between Dubois's clenched teeth, his eyes ignited, and he half rose from his chair.

"That's preposterous! What are you idiots trying to do, ruin me? Bankrupt me? Go back and start over; you'll get the correct total to the penny or you'll stay here till you do; if you stay all night. Is that clear?"

"Sir, my wife and I are invited to a birthday party tonight. We're supposed to be there at six. It's almost five."

"I don't care if you're invited to the coronation of Queen Victoria, get back to your stool and get busy! If you clear this up before six, consider yourself lucky; you'll at least be able to show up, even if you are late. If you don't, you may lose more than a night out, do I make myself clear?"

"But my wife..."

"The devil take her! Let her go alone. Get back to work! Ow, oooo, that hurt. Now see what you've made me do! Out! I don't want to see your face again until you're balanced!"

• • •

Adrienne stared fixedly at Raider. Then she averted her eyes and shook her head.

"Of all the stupid..."

"What? Me comin' t' take you back? What's stupid 'bout it? Your husband's worried sick. He can't see straight, he's so worried. Can't eat, can't sleep."

"You've walked right into the lion's den; what do you have, a death wish?"

"I'm a Pinkerton, ma'am, it's my job. We don't get to choose, I was assigned. We only got a few minutes. Let's not talk 'bout me. We gotta get both of us outta here. I got a plan; pay 'tention."

"You're wasting your time."

His head jerked back like a chicken's; disbelief flooded his features. He hadn't heard her right.

"I'm not leaving."

"The hell you're not. You may not've caught on, but you're in big danger here. I mean really big. These boys can turn on you in a split second. No need t' draw pictures, I'll just remind you what they did to Fanny Kelly, Mrs. Oatman, and a lotta others."

"I refuse to leave my husband."

"Jesus Chri... I mean what in hell did they do, hit you over the head an' jangle your brains? Your poor husband's sittin' back in Collardsville waitin' for you, prayin' I can get you out."

"My husband is just outside. He-Dog is my husband."

Raider's jaw dropped.

"I have no other," she went on.

He read the situation immediately and correctly. He-Dog had been sleeping with her and she liked it; so much that all thoughts of Edgar had vanished. The stink, the jabbering, the primitive life, the rotten food, all of it was endurable when balanced on the scales against He-Dog's manhood. It was rare, but it did happen that a captured white woman became so enamored of her abductor that she lost all perspective, all common sense. She began to live for the nights and his embrace; sex was all that mattered, and evidently He-Dog was six times the man Edgar was and she loved every minute of it.

"You're talkin' very foolish," he said quietly. "You don't b'long here, the women don't want you, an' the other braves don't. You got a husband that worships you back there in civ'lization. He loves you, you love him, you know you do."

"I know nothing of the kind. It may shock you to hear it, but I've never loved him. How could any woman? He's so in love with himself, he couldn't possibly love me, he doesn't know how to give of himself, he's cold, unfeeling, demanding..."

"So how come you married 'im?"

"None of your business."

"On account he's rich," Raider accused.

"I said none of your business!" She started for the mouth of the cave. "That's all, we have nothing more to talk about. I wish you luck, I hope they'll let you ride out of here without scalping you. If you have any sense at all, you'll politely ask Crazy Horse if he'll allow you to. He seems to like you, or at least respect you. Tell him you want to leave, he may oblige you."

"I'm not goin' anyplace without you."

"You're being very stupid. I know; just doing your job."

He was sitting on the floor. She had come back from the entrance. She stood, hands on hips, looking down at him in the dim light.

"You don't understand, do you. I'm sorry, it's not your fault, you'd have to be a woman to."

"I understand. You like sleepin' with He-Dog."

She glared. "You're as disgusting as you are stupid."

"I'm sorry, I got no right to judge anybody. Look, be sensible, use your head before you get both of us scalped."

"I'm in no danger."

"That's what *you* think..."

"I'm not. He-Dog, Arthur, has sworn to protect me."

"Ar..."

"My father's name was Arthur."

She knelt, capping her knees with her hands, and searched his eyes for understanding.

"Let me tell you something. That day when I was out berrying and they kidnapped me I was on the verge of leaving Edgar. I'd had all I could stand of his demanding, his snobbishness, his coldness, his pawing and slobbering. I made up my mind that as soon as I got back to town I would go to Emil Franz, the lawyer, and file for divorce. Then, while I stood there picking, actually deciding, fate stepped in. They kidnapped me, brought me here..."

"An' you love it. It's your friggin' garden o' Eden; you're Eve an' he's Adam."

"Think what you like, your opinion doesn't interest me in the slightest."

"It damn well better, lady. Let me tell you something, maybe you do think you found happiness, maybe you do think you can hack it, but you can't. It's too rough a life. You had it too soft, too easy, to put up with what these boys put up with. Be honest, the first couplea days you couldn't even keep the damn food down; you tossed up everything you ate."

"Not now."

"You cut yourself, get infected, you get really sick, who'll take care o' you? Where you gonna get a doctor out here, Chrissakes?"

"I can take care of myself. The Indians have no need for any doctor."

"You're no Injun, you'll find out, Mrs. Know-it-All. The—whatcha'callit—novelty'll wear off. Winter'll come on, they'll move out an' over t' the Powder River. There'll be fightin' with the Crows, the Shoshones, the Pawnees; these boys can't get along with nobody, 'Cept maybe the other Sioux tribes. And wait'll the army comes after 'em.

"Tell you something else, I bet you dollars t' doughnuts He-Dog won't stick by you. He's a good lookin' fella, plenty o' young girls'd give their braids an' everythin' else to lay with 'im...."

She laughed. But, he noticed, it was a little hollow, a

little forced. "You think you know him, you don't know anything about him."

"You think you do?" he snapped. "You think you can know any Injun? You got the wrong color skin, lady. What's the matter with you? All right, so you don't love your husband. . . ."

"Edgar? Love? Are you insane?"

"That's no reason t' stay here. Come back with me an' divorce 'im if that's what you want. Leave, leave Nebraska, go back t' Boston. . . ."

"Hartford, Connecticut."

"But don't do this t' yourself."

"Why shouldn't I? Why can't I do what I want? It's my life, isn't it?"

"You don't know what you're bitin' off here."

"I'm learning, and the more I see, the surer I am I've made a wise decision."

"Stupid decision."

He-Dog filled the entrance. She heard him coming, rose, turned, and went out with him. Left alone, Raider sent his hand down his trouserleg, satisfying himself that the Sharps was still in place, loaded, available, though what possible use four shots would be against so many braves proved a realization sufficiently dismaying to drop his face into a frown.

He considered the situation as dispassionately as his mounting annoyance with Adrienne Dubois permitted. Clearly, he couldn't talk her into changing her mind and coming with him. In large measure he could blame Edgar for that. If he'd been half the man He-Dog was she might think twice about staying, volunteering to turn white squaw.

"If she won't come o' her own free will, I'm gonna hafta kidnap her back."

He groaned. It would be tough enough getting himself out with his hide intact without fetching her along, probably kicking and screaming. She was loony, a touch of the sun, had to be. No woman in her right mind would swap a life like hers for this, and she wasn't thinking with her mind. What she was thinking with was located a lot lower in her anatomy.

He could kick himself blue for messing up with Crazy Horse; coming to the Black Hills posing as a gewgaw salesman. He should have started with his other strategy, announcing he was representing Governor Furnas, threatening reprisal from the army, requesting, not demanding, they hand her over and let them leave. At that, what difference did it make? She refused to go anyway.

He chuckled cynically, recalling thinking earlier that all he really needed was a generous slab of luck. He'd gotten it all right, slab on slab, all bad.

CHAPTER ELEVEN

Raider was placed untied in a cave of his own to await Crazy Horse's decision as to what should be done with him. It crossed his mind that all things considered it might be the most sensible course to try to escape and leave her. That's what she wanted. Who was he to deny her?

It crossed his mind but the idea did not linger there. He couldn't possibly leave her. Pinkerton would come down on him like a falling wall. Her husband would raise holy hell; that didn't worry him, nor for that matter did Pinkerton's certain reaction. Unfortunately, there was a principle involved that he could not lose sight of. A company of roving savages is no company for a white woman, any white woman, much less the delicate product of a Connecticut finishing school who'd been waited on hand and foot all her life.

"I gotta get her outta here whether she likes it or not. An' she won't. She'll likely turn into a she-cougar, all claws an' teeth, when I try."

Of course he could always put her to sleep. By the time she came around he'd be halfway to the Hotalings' place and out of danger. He snorted. How, he wondered, could he make something that was patently so hard sound so easy?

"Halfway to the Hotalings? Hell, I'll be lucky t' get a hunnert yards!"

And if he did try and failed it would be tantamount to signing his own death warrant. Crazy Horse's liking, his respect, whatever it was he felt for Raider, would vanish like fog over a swamp when the sun comes out. He'd see it as ungratefulness and would order up two poles and a crossbar and turn loose the squaws.

"They'd kill me certain. Jesus, that'd be all I need!"

Black as the sky can get, sooner or later a little light is bound to shine through. And so it was with Crazy Horse's prisoner. Three days after Raider was brought in and Adrienne flatly refused his offer to rescue her, she came to visit him.

"How are you?" she asked solicitously.

"Oh, aces, never better. Vacation's 'zactly what I need. Comfortable room, good food, friendly companionship, rotten stinks."

"I have been talking about you to Arthur."

"His name is He-Dog."

"He likes me to call him Arthur, it amuses him; besides, it's none of your business. Are you going to listen to me?"

"You're gonna help me get away."

She looked surprised. "How did you know that?"

"I saw it in the tea leaves this mornin' at breakfast."

"You are the most sarcastic man I have ever met. Yes, I'm going to help you escape. For both our sakes. You'll get free and live to tell of it, and I'll get you out of my hair. Arthur was dead against your getting away, he prefers to see you executed, but I've talked and talked to him and he's finally come around to my way of thinking. Doesn't that surprise you? That he respects me enough to listen to me? It's more than dear Edgar ever did."

Raider thought of something venomously sarcastic, but he held his tongue.

"Arthur has agreed to talk to Crazy Horse on your behalf."

"Favor to you." He sniffed and looked away.

"Not for you."

"What do I have t' do?"

"Absolutely nothing. Oh, in the interest of, shall I say diplomacy, we mustn't be too conspicuous about it. Tonight after the others are asleep I'll come back and take you to your horse. You'll get on it and leave."

"Good, sounds fine."

She slitted her eyes suspiciously. "Don't try anything funny or I guarantee you'll only get yourself killed."

"Hey, funny's the furthest thing from my mind." He nodded sharply.

"It had better be."

"You're sure you don't wanta come with me?" he asked, his tone exaggeratedly innocent.

"I don't even want to discuss it. No point. I'll come back around midnight. Arthur will come, too."

"How come? What for?"

"That worries you? We're saving your life, Mr. Weatherbee; you might show a little less curiosity and a little more gratitude."

"Right. Thanks."

"See you later."

This was not the light showing through the blackness of Raider's dilemma. It appeared shortly after sundown as the Indians were preparing for their evening meal. Down from the north came a hundred warriors, Crows from the look of them, the Absaroke from their long unbraided hair and porcupine quill bibs. And the fact that all the other tribes surrounding the Black Hills were either blood brothers to the Oglala, fellow Sioux, or allies like the Cheyenne. Or even the peaceful Shoshone, who wanted no part of the Oglalas. These had to be Crows and they were a long way from their hunting grounds in Montana, probably just passing through. But having accidentally come upon the Oglalas, they were not disposed to continue on. Now right away.

Though far fewer, they caught the Oglalas completely by surprise, an advantage the Crows lost no time in exploiting. Raider was stretched out on the floor of his cave relaxing and ruminating on his situation when he heard shouting and sporadic gunfire. He ran to the entrance. The sun was blood red, perched on the horizon. The air was still but the north side of the camp was blue with smoke. The attackers carried more rifles than any hostile tribe should; it looked as if every man was armed with one. Confusion and terror reigned. Crazy Horse stood before his cave shouting commands, attempting to collect his men. If all the Siouan tribes had one fault in common it was that they fought not for the unit, but for individual glory. From what Raider could see at first glance, Crazy Horse was doing his best to change his warrior's philosophy of strategy in sixty seconds. The women and children streamed into the protection of the caves, screaming loudly. He could not see Adrienne anywhere, but He-Dog and two other men obeyed Crazy Horse and came running to join him.

Raider thought a moment and reached a decision. He could probably easily get away during the action, but he couldn't take Adrienne with him; at the moment he didn't even know where she was. Still, if he stayed and joined his captors in fighting off their attackers, whatever warm feelings Crazy Horse already had for him, if indeed he had any, would measurably increase. He might not appreciate Raider's sneakiness in hiding the Sharps, but if he managed to knock off a couple of Crows, Crazy Horse would be quick to forgive him.

He got the little gun out and the sack of shells for it he'd slipped down inside his left boot and had worn all the way from Collardsville. The Sharps was fully loaded, all four chambers. He ran forward, crouched behind the first rock he came to, and eased carefully around it for a quick look. The Crows were circling the camp like they would a prairie wagon train, one-handing their rifles, firing under their horses' necks Comanche-style, screaming like stricken banshees. Raider moved from cover to cover to get closer to the moving circle, finding and crouching behind a convenient outcropping providing him a range of about fifteen feet. Any farther away he wouldn't hit a thing, so woefully inaccurate was the little weapon at .44 or .45 range.

He potted two hostiles in quick succession, the second dropped screaming from his pony. Raider almost laughed at the sound of the little gun; it popped like a toy gun. But, unlike a toy, it killed.

The Crows' circle was beginning to break up now, not because the Oglalas were turning the tables, but because the attackers were seeking better cover than their ponies' heads. When they dismounted they changed weapons and began lofting arrows into the camp. One came singing down, imbedding itself less than six inches from Raider's left boot. Suddenly it was raining arrows, and enough rifle fire continued to pour into the camp to keep the defenders' heads down.

Raider glanced behind him. Crazy Horse was still standing just inside the cave entrance. His lieutenants had dispersed, his braves having quickly taken up their positions. He noticed Raider and raised his hand, then moved inside the cave.

The Sharps missed with the last two shots of its load. *He* didn't miss, Raider assured himself, he was a terrific shot. It was the fault of the little weapon. It was reliable at four feet, ten was stretching its range, and at fifteen feet he figured the odds three to one against hitting a target the size of a man. He reloaded and resumed firing, steadying his wrist with his free hand. An arrow clattered off one side of his rock, a slug ricochetted off the other. He ducked, cursed, and rested his weapon. A loud clamoring rising above the sound of the gunfire caught his attention directly behind him. The squaws, children, and old people were emerging from their cover and heading for the cave into which Crazy Horse had vanished minutes before, leaving cooking pots, baskets, blankets, food, everything. Crazy Horse had probably given the order to move out, reasoned Raider.

"Only where in hell are they gonna move to?" he wondered aloud.

The Crows had surrounded the camp. Attempting to break through their circle would be suicide. Again he rested the Sharps and watched the people fall all over each other in their haste to get inside. In seconds the cave had swallowed them all, leaving the men to fight on.

The battle was too one-sided to give even the most optimistic Oglala reason for hope. In twos and threes Crazy Horse's warriors began to retreat toward the cave entrance, reaching and backing into it until fewer than fifteen defenders remained among the clutter and disarray and the bodies of the slain.

Raider resumed firing, taking down three more Crows and drawing more attention from them than any of the Oglalas. They had to be surprised to come upon a white man fighting with their blood enemy. Which set him to wondering where the white woman had gone. By now the crimson sun had all but completely vanished below the horizon over the distant Laramies. Suddenly, out of nowhere, came He-Dog, dodging arrows and scurrying up to him.

"You come..."

"What are you talkin' 'bout? What the hell's goin' on? Why's everybody hidin' in that one cave? Chrissakes, everybody runs in there they'll pile grass at the mouth, smoke you out, pot you like bottles off a rail fence. Either that or fill the dark fulla lead."

"You come," repeated He-Dog sternly, grabbing him by the arm.

Raider shook him off. "Lemme be. You wanna wind up feedin' the circlin' birds, go ahead. Not me. I got 'bout sixty shots left and I'm gonna get me fifty-eight of 'em 'fore they get me. So beat it."

"Cave open inside end. Far from here." He swung his arm. A descending arrow nearly skinned it. He ignored it as he would a fly. "Over behind those hills."

"How 'bout that. Pretty slick..."

He glanced past him at the entrance to the cave. The few remaining defenders were backing toward it, the last four, actually. As he watched two were hit and went down, writhing in the dust, lying still. He-Dog started off. Crouching, Raider watched He-Dog dodge from cover to cover until he was almost up to the cave. There he stopped, turned, and looked back, waving for Raider to follow.

A mistake.

An arrow came whirring down. His attention on Raider, He-Dog failed to see it. It struck him in the crotch, causing him to scream so loudly, so chillingly, Raider's spine tingled. He stiffened and watched him grab his crotch with one hand. Blood showed through his fingers. Then he staggered backward into the cave and out of sight.

"Holy crow," murmured Raider.

He emitted a low whistle and holstered his gun. He started off following the route rock by rock that He-Dog had taken, praying for better luck in reaching the cave.

"I sure 'nough do feel for you, Arthur. Damn, that must feel like your jewels bein' torched."

Night had descended by the time the first echelon of the fleeing tribe emerged into the open air. Threading his way through the pitch darkness, Raider stumbled upon He-Dog and Adrienne. Recognizing her voice when he practically fell over her, Raider lit his last match. He-Dog lay prone; she was ministering to him, wiping the blood from his crotch with the hem of her skirt. He was in absolute agony.

"Help us..." she whispered pleadingly.

He took one look and swallowed. The arrow had struck with unerring accuracy. Its target was beyond help. He-Dog would never please his new "bride" again, never please any woman.

Raider stopped a brave making his way along the wall past them. Together they carried the suffering He-Dog to the mouth of the cave and out into the open. By this time his excruciating pain had caused him to pass out. He had lost a lot of blood. Adrienne ripped strips from her skirt and bandaged the wound as best she could. Crazy Horse joined them. Raider explained what had happened. The chief grunted in reaction. There was no sympathy in his expression; his friend's misfortune was not his own, decided Raider, studying him, and therefore no concern of his. Other problems took precedence.

He wondered what was passing through Adrienne's

mind at that moment. Was life among the savages still so fascinating, so attractive? His attention moved from Crazy Horse to her. She knelt beside her lover, clutching her breasts with her forearms, moving her trunk up and down, sobbing loudly. He-Dog slept on, his suffering etched on his handsome face.

CHAPTER TWELVE

A litter was fashioned to carry the wounded He-Dog to the tribe's new campsite about four miles to the east. His pain persisted. Hitewa, the gnarled and ancient medicine man, took over for Adrienne. He brought his bag of secret conjures and talismans to drive away the evil spirits and rid the patient's body of bad medicine. Among the tools of his trade, used to the accompaniment of chants, drumming, and gourd rattling, were dried human fingers, deer tails, and a small sack of curative herbs. He mixed a number of them in a shallow bowl, added water to make a poultice, and applied it to his patient's crotch.

"I don't know what it is," said Adrienne to Raider as they stood together watching. "But if it eases his pain..."

"It's prob'ly got skullcap and willow bark juice in it."

"You know a lot about the Indians and their ways, don't you?"

"I been out here a long time; gotta pick up a few things."

"You do know a lot. Crazy Horse seems to sense it, which is probably why he admires you. At least he respects you."

"I don't see much o' either."

"If he didn't, he'd have trussed you up and hung you like he did those three prospectors."

"What *about* those three?"

"What do you mean?"

"What d'you think? You think the Injuns were right to murder 'em?"

"They trespassed on their sacred lands."

"Is that somethin' you murder a man for? Why not chase 'em off?"

"You're overlooking a very important point. They didn't just murder them. They hung them up in a clear view. As a warning to the other prospectors. If they have the sense God gave them at birth they'll get out and stay out."

"A man don't exercise much sense where gold's concerned. You stick common sense an' greed in the same barrel to duke it out an' greed'll win every time. Besides, the prospectors know they got the federal gover'ment behind 'em, the army."

"These hills are Sioux land by treaty. The U.S. government would hardly make a treaty, then turn around and deliberately break it."

"Oh my no, that'd be downright shameful."

"There's no need to be sarcastic."

"Let me tell you somethin', Missus Dubois, these Injuns, all Injuns, may be noble savages, courageous underdogs, children o' the earth, God's best handiwork, and fun to sleep with, but they're doomed. Their days are numbered. The white man's got the power over 'em and there's no way he's gonna give it up. White people want the Injuns' land, their buffalo, their gold an' silver, everything they got, and they won't rest till they get 'em. Crazy Horse can hang up fifty prospectors, a hundred more'll come t' take their place, an' five hundred after 'em. You, lady, are backin' the wrong horse, which I don't mean as a joke. You better get wise t' yourself in a hurry and"—he lowered his voice—"quit this fun an' games you got yourself into, an' come with me."

"And desert poor Arthur? Don't be a ninny."

"One of us is a ninny. I'm not sure it's me."

"And if I did leave, where would I go? Back to Edgar? Not a chance. Never."

"Don't. Hey, I met 'im, I know what you're talkin' 'bout. My point is get outta here. Go back to civ'lization. Go to Hartford, go to Omaha, Santa Fe, anyplace, but don't stay here."

"I simply cannot desert him. A wife's place is by her husband's side."

"Sure, like old Edgar's," he murmured.

"What did you say?"

"Nothin'."

Silence ensued between them; their eyes met and locked. She was the first to resume speaking.

"Will you be leaving?" she asked in a low voice.

"Not without you."

"I'll never leave, never. If I spend the next fifty years here, every year, every day will be preferable to back there. We love each other too deeply for me to think only of myself. I could never."

"You better start, an' soon."

Crazy Horse came up, holding his hand out. He didn't demand the Sharps, he didn't have to, Raider understood. He lifted it from its holster and handed it to him.

"And the ammunition."

He complied.

"You're welcome," said Raider tightly.

Crazy Horse furrowed his brow questioningly.

"I killed at least ten or eleven Crows and you show your 'preciation by takin' my gun away," growled Raider. "Thanks a lot."

Crazy Horse smiled a rare smile. "If you need it, come and ask me for it."

"Sure. We gonna stay here?"

"We are safe here for the time being. There is water, good natural protection, caves. The Crows have not found us and probably won't. I have sent two men back to watch them. Tomorrow others will go back and fetch our ponies. They were well hidden; the Crows will not find them. I don't worry about the ponies or the Crows, I worry about you. What am I to do with you?"

"I killed fourteen or fifteen of 'em for you back there, you should fall all over me with gratefulness. Better yet, just let me leave an' take her."

"No!" burst Adrienne.

"She does not seem to want to go," said Crazy Horse

leering. He glanced toward the prostrate, still sleeping He-Dog. The medicine man had finished treating him and had left. "When He-Dog awakens, ask him if he will give her up, why don't you?"

"Sure."

For the next seven days Raider bided his time. He did not discuss leaving and taking Adrienne with either Crazy Horse or with her. He saw little of her, so busy was she tending to He-Dog. He was on the mend. His pain had all but completely gone, the bleeding had stopped, and by the seventh day he was able to get about, although with obvious difficulty. Crazy Horse approached Raider to talk about his friend. Raider was surprised at his concern, his change of heart. He didn't think anybody's troubles, regardless of how bad, would interest the chief. Stoicism and aloofness, after all, were important to his image. Still, He-Dog *was* his best friend. Evidently something resembling compassion had sneaked into Crazy Horse's heart. Why he permitted it to quickly became apparent.

"His manhood is destroyed."

"It looked it."

"I did not know when it happened that the arrow severed his thing. There was so much blood..."

"Poor bastard."

"Poor bastard. Hitewa says that he will recover, but will never lie with his woman again."

"That's for sure."

"He will be a man in every respect but one. He will be like a *berdache*."

Raider recognized the word for homosexual. Crazy Horse was right, he would be. Whether or not he'd take to wearing a berdache dress remained to be seen, but Raider strongly doubted it. Such attire silently proclaimed the wearer's sexual preference to all who recognized it. Indians believed the moon appeared to boys during puberty and offered a bow and a woman's pack strap. If the boy hesitated when reaching for the bow, the moon handed him the pack strap, symbolizing a feminized life-style. Berdaches served the tribe as matchmakers and often went into battle unarmed to treat wounded warriors.

But even deprived as he was, He-Dog was too much a man to adopt the life and ways of a berdache. If the temptation visited him he would kill himself.

"Poor bastard," repeated Crazy Horse and walked off, bouncing the little sack of .22 caliber ammunition up and down in his palm like a ball.

That night Adrienne came to Raider, waking him. He shot up to a sitting position.

"Whatsa matter?"

"Shhh, keep your voice down, we mustn't wake the others."

His heart beat faster. She had changed her mind. It had to be. He-Dog was no longer of any use to her. It had been seven nights since she'd felt him inside her. To go from so much fornication to none at all she must be boiling inside.

"We can get out tonight," he said. "There's no moon. Nobody watchin' the ponies. We can grab my mare and one for you an' rattle our hocks. Be down close t' the border by sunup..."

"Shhhhh! No. I'm not leaving. How many times do I have to tell you? Can't you get it through that thick head of yours?"

"So whatta you want?"

"Get up, come with me."

"To where?"

She pointed. "That cave is empty. That is, nobody's sleeping there. They're using it to store weapons. Come, we have to talk."

" 'Bout what?"

"Just come!" she rasped irritably and reached for his hand.

Four blankets lay on the floor of the cave. At sight of them in the feeble light of the dying fire outside she squeezed his hand. He understood, he sighed aloud.

"What's the matter?"

"Adrienne, Missus Dubois."

"Adrienne, why so formal? Stop, stand there."

She began unbuttoning his trousers. He protested. She ignored him. Almost before he realized it they were down and she was working his member with her hand. Suddenly possessed, on fire with lust for him, pulling at him so hard he yelped in pain. She quieted him with her mouth, clamping it tightly against his, driving her tongue at his.

He scarcely knew how it came about so mesmerized was he by her behavior, her wildness. She was an animal; eager, dying to rut, to get him inside her, and when he did mount her and thrust forward, she squealed with joy and began bucking furiously.

"Fuck me! Fuck me! Fuck me! Fuck me!"

CHAPTER THIRTEEN

Crazy Horse summoned Raider around noon the next day. He proceeded to astonish Raider, telling him that he knew what had happened in the privacy of the storage cave the night before, that everyone in camp knew about it.

"He-Dog knows and wants you dead."

Raider quickly recovered from his surprise. "Is killin' me gonna give the poor bastard back his manhood? Understand somethin', I didn't attack her, it was the other way round."

Crazy Horse grinned. "Is that the way it is with you white people?"

"I'm bein' serious!"

"So is He-Dog. You have committed a crime which cannot be forgiven."

"Shit, what about her?"

"She is just a woman, a thing to be enjoyed and put aside, ignored when not wanted."

"How come..."

He stopped. He wanted to remind Crazy Horse of all the squaws whose noses were cut off by their men when they were caught fornicating, but putting the thing on Adrienne wouldn't take it off him. Not in He-Dog's eyes. Besides, if he ever did get around to bringing her back to Collardsville and her loving husband, he certainly didn't want to present her with her pretty nose sliced off. Crazy Horse was eyeing him with a puzzled expression, obviously wondering why Raider didn't continue speaking.

"Never mind," mumbled Raider.

"I am not stupid, Weatherbee, or blind. I know who is at fault in this, but you are not innocent. You helped me with the Crows and for that we are all grateful. You are not like the gold stealers that we captured and punished. You deserve better. As does He-Dog, even if he does not realize it."

"I don't foller you."

"His heart is shattered, he is destroyed as a man. No man wants to be the object of pity, but that is what he is. Whatever his condition, whatever his problems, he is still my good friend. What he needs now more than anything else is the chance to display his manhood. Show his bravery and quiet the tongues. Kill the rat of pity. I have decided. You and He-Dog will duel. If he wins, he will win respect. If he loses, he will die admired and remembered."

"What kinda duel?"

"Knives. With the wrists of your left hands and right ankles joined by strips of rawhide."

"Oh, Chrissakes..."

"Chrissakes?"

"Nothin'. Is that what he wants?"

"It is what I want. And you. Or would you prefer to hang upside down and be stoned to death by the squaws?"

"Yeah..."

Raider only half heard him, he had suddenly plunged into thought. Crazy Horse's right eyebrow arched.

"You would?"

"No! When?"

"That will be for him to decide. His injury is not yet healed. Perhaps he will want another day or two. In the meantime..." He lifted his hand and motioned reprovingly with his index finger. "You will stay away from his woman."

"Hey, tell her t' stay away from me, why don'cha?"

"If you are found with her, you will be executed on the spot."

"You mind tellin' her that? At least in the damn duel, I'll stand half a friggin' chance."

He raised his voice for the last few words; he had to. Crazy Horse suddenly took it into his head to walk away.

Late that afternoon Adrienne came upon him sitting on a rock turning over his rapidly multiplying problems, discarding one after another without reaching a solution. At sight of her he jumped up.

"What's the matter?" she asked.

"Get outta here, lemme alone. Anybody see us together, they'll chop me down like ripe wheat."

"Don't be silly, nobody'll see us up here."

He looked about them worriedly. From where they stood, they could not see a single Oglala below.

"We have to talk," she went on.

"Yeah, yeah, you allus want t' talk, but nothin' ever really gets said. Jesus Christ, I hope you're proud o' yourself. You got me into the soup up to my friggin' neck. Crazy Horse wants me an' Arthur t' fight a damn duel."

"What are you talking about?"

He explained. She listened, wide-eyed. She began shaking her head.

"You and he can't fight a duel, he's in no condition. Besides, you're being even stupider than usual. What you should be doing is getting out of here."

"I keep tellin' you . . ."

"Not without me, I know."

She sat on a rock looking at him. "I feel sorry for you. I really do."

"Me, too."

"You talk about the Indians fighting a losing battle. What about you? You never should have come after me and now that you're here, it's stupid to stay. If you walked down to the horses, got on yours and rode away, nobody would even bother turning to look, much less stop you. Except of course Arthur. Crazy Horse wouldn't."

As she talked she looked about them. Her eyes lit on a patch of sun-withered grass between two boulders. Beyond it rose a grove of pine trees. He read her mind as she suddenly stopped talking. Read her eyes.

"Oh no you don't..."

She seized his hand. "Come, you know you want to."

"You're nuts, you know that?"

He jerked free and started off. She called after him.

"Coward! You're pathetic, you know that!"

"Yeah," he grumbled, "that's me. I must be, t' stick round waitin' for you t' change your goddamn mind...."

He-Dog wanted no postponement, declaring himself completely recovered, fit, and ready to fight. At Crazy Horse's direction two braves drew a circle on the ground about twenty feet in diameter. Rawhide strips were provided, two, both about four feet in length. Raider's and He-Dog's left wrists were joined with one, their right ankles with the other. Raider was given a knife. He was quick to notice that the blade of his knife was at least an inch and a half shorter than his adversary's. He protested. A chorus of laughter went up, led by Crazy Horse, as both men stripped to the waist.

"So much for your friggin' noble savage," muttered Raider.

In the crowd that closed around the circle he did not see Adrienne. He decided that she probably couldn't bear to watch for fear that He-Dog would be injured or killed. She certainly wasn't worried about him, he thought.

All eyes were on Crazy Horse as he lifted his right arm, fingers upward, held it, then brought it down sharply.

Both men crouched and began slowly circling, eyes riveted on each other, He-Dog's lip curled with hatred, his expression glowering, eyes flinging the fire of his anger. Which was good, thought Raider, a man fighting while consumed with emotion was apt to be impulsive, careless, impatient to get it over with.

He-Dog thrust, Raider dodged. Adroitly, only just not quickly enough. He-Dog's gleaming blade skinned the Pinkerton's rib wound, opening it slightly; he could feel the bleeding start. Not badly, not enough to worry about, but enough to draw an encouraging cheer from the onlookers. He-Dog leered. Again he thrust; Raider countered, pricking him in the breastbone, drawing blood. He-Dog's leer collapsed into a glare.

"Tit for tat, Arthur," murmured Raider.

He wondered why he could not generate the urge to kill He-Dog, to even harm him just enough to end the damned thing. He knew why; he felt sorry for the poor bastard. He was the victim of a fluke accident; now that Raider thought about it, it might have been better if the arrow had lodged in his heart. And this stupid duel wasn't He-Dog's doing, wasn't even Crazy Horse's.

It was hers and she didn't even have the decency to watch it, although what decency it took he had no idea. More like guts. Women! If they didn't get a man into the soup nine times out of ten, they got him eight. Why the hell did she go out berry picking in the first place, out that far from the protection of the town? It was almost as if she *wanted* to be grabbed. Maybe she did.

What's the matter with me? mused Raider. *This boy's out to gut me proper, what am I thinkin' 'bout her for?*

He-Dog lunged and missed, throwing himself badly off balance, passing Raider on the right as he sidestepped the Indian. He-Dog bent his upper body, and for a split second placed himself at Raider's mercy. Raider eyed his exposed back. All he had to do was lift his hand and plunge his knife straight down.

But he did not and He-Dog's forward motion jerked the rawhide binding them, pulling Raider to his right and dispatching his chance to end it then and there. He cursed aloud his failure to thrust, but it was too late now. He-Dog quickly righted himself, turning, and coming back at him, slashing wildly. Raider feinted and ducked, managing to keep clear of the flashing blade, at times by the narrowest of margins. Once the edge hit the heel of his upraised hand, opening a mouth in the soft flesh, drooling blood. It plopped in the sand at his feet.

The onlookers oohed and ahed with every thrust, every

move, even when one or the other just shifted his feet. And when blood showed they cheered. The sun was broiling hot; Raider was sweating like a pig, its salt stung his eyes and once momentarily blinded him.

He-Dog was no better off. In fact worse; his heart was in the fight and he hungered for vengeance, but his body wasn't up to it and he was rapidly tiring. Not his movements but his face betrayed him. His jaw muscles stretched tauter and tauter, his lips stretched over his teeth, sweat poured from every pore and his eyes were taking on a sickly yellow hue. His expression clearly displayed his waning confidence. His nerves were flailing his muscles, tiring, weakening them. Again and again he swiped sweat from his forehead with his free hand.

Another furious burst, sudden energy-depleting exertion, and his knees would begin to wobble. That, Raider knew, would be the beginning of the end.

They feinted and slashed air. Twice their blades struck. Once He-Dog penetrated Raider's defense enough to get him with the tip of his blade, leaving a large, thin, bloody X on his chest. Raider retaliated, sidestepping a lunge and slashing the top of the Indian's wrist. Sight of his own blood infuriated He-Dog; he feinted awkwardly, like a marionette jerked by invisible strings. He swung his knife wildly, switching it from hand to hand; a dangerous move, but one that imbued his thrusting with a fresh surge of power and gave his right arm a chance to recover from its exhaustion.

Suddenly Adrienne broke through the circle behind He-Dog. Raider raised his eyes at the sight of her and as he did so she smiled, touching the tip of her tongue to her upper lip, and nodding. A nod of encouragement. A nod that urged him to win, to defeat, to kill.

"Bitch..." he rasped.

He-Dog reacted in surprise. He half-turned his head to see what Raider was looking at. A tactical mistake, a terrible mistake. Raider lunged; sensing it coming, warned by his instincts. He-Dog tried to evade it. He managed to, swinging sideways and sucking his stomach in, but executing the move so awkwardly, without properly repositioning his feet to maintain his balance, that he began to fall to his right. The crowd gasped and oohed. Down he went, rolling over, snapping the rawhide strip joining his and Raider's wrists, coming to rest on his back. Raider straddled him; bending, setting the point of his knife against his throat. He-Dog's eyes rounded with fear. He lay perfectly still, holding his breath. Not a whisper, not a sound issued from the onlookers. Raider's whole body knotted as he stared down at his helpless foe. Every instinct in him ordered him to push the blade home, drive it deep into He-Dog's throat. His brain dispatched the command to his shoulder to drive downward pushing his forearm, his wrist, his fist, the knife. Thrust! Kill! He growled in frustration. His arm shook. It was as if an invisible shield had inserted itself between point and flesh. Raider's sweat dripped and splashed on He-Dog's chest and still the sickened eyes gaped in horror, still Raider's arm quivered, still his knuckles whitened paler, paler, still he could not bring himself to finish him off.

"*Chamota latia!*" burst He-Dog.

Before Raider could move, he shot both hands upward, seized Raider's fist which gripped the knife and with a scream, pulled it hilt deep into his throat.

CHAPTER FOURTEEN

The two scouts sat their saddles studying the grisly scene. The stench of rotting corpses came wafting toward them, carried on the breeze coming down from the caves. It swung the three hanging prospectors' bodies gently and rustled the pine trees marshaled east of the site like a green legion preparing to advance.

The taller and older of the two men, Lacroix, cleared his throat, spat, and shook his head. In his veins French and Shoshone-Bannock blood commingled in equal parts. He had been an army scout attached to Fort Meade for the past two years. Before that he had trapped in the Bitterroots in Montana for years. Lately he had been entertaining notions of trying his hand at prospecting. There was gold in these hills and if he intended to go after his share he'd better make a move soon. By next spring the Black Hills would be swarming with pocket hunters. Gold fever was the "catchingest disease known to man." Oh my yes, there was gold here. It was said that when the men building the Gordon Stockade near French Creek dug an eight-foot-deep hole in one corner to set a post they found it. Only one thing gave Lacroix pause before changing careers: The sight before his eyes, the punishment meted out by the Sioux to white men who invaded their sacred lands.

His companion was ten years younger than Lacroix. His name was Bishop and he had only been scouting for the army for about six months. But he knew the area, having been born and grown up in Deadwood up north on Whitewood Creek. He was a superb scout, he knew the Indians and their ways and minds as well as his partner, though unlike Lacroix he had no Indian blood in him.

Both wore civilian clothes as befit their jobs. They worked for the army, took their orders from officers and were paid by the paymaster, but had never sworn to defend their country and the length of their "enlistments" was theirs to stipulate. The only outward indication attesting to their association with the military was their belts. Both wore the regulation plain black glazed leather officer's belt bearing a belt-plate of yellow gilt over their jackets.

Shading his eyes, Lacroix continued to study the carnage. And screwed up his badly broken nose at the stink.

"Go on back and tell the captain. I'll have a look around."

"Man, it stinks. Makes ya' sick." Bishop grimaced and stuck his tongue out.

"The breeze is coming straight down. Go on..."

Ten minutes later Captain Willis Carpenter came trotting up at the head of the column. The guidon bearer rested the flapping guidon, driving the pole into the soft ground. The guidon bore the legend Fifth Cavalry. At Carpenter's command B Troop dismounted. He was a heavy-set man in his mid-fifties, a singularly unmilitary looking soldier. Indeed, he looked as if his middle should be swathed in an apron and he should be standing behind a counter in his properly gartered shirtsleeves, no tie, but with a straw hat crowning his round head. He removed his gloves, paired them neatly and stuffed them in his belt. He called and waved to Lacroix who was moving about up by the mouth of the largest cave. The scout came loping down.

"What did you find?"

"Oglalas. From the look of things they camped here some time, maybe a month or two. Strange for Oglalas, they are the movin'est Sioux in the whole West."

He produced a strip of bearskin with six feathers attached to it from inside his shirt, handing it to the captain.

"Oglala?"

"No, sir, Crow. Part of a Crow war bonnet. Crows always use bear fur in their bonnets and they don't cut notches or slice the eagle feathers like the Sioux do. The

Crow thinks the grizzly is his personal bodyguard..."

"Yes, yes..."

Carpenter did not want a lecture on the ways of the Crow, not at the moment, not with his officers and men looking on and listening.

"What do you make of it?" he asked.

"They came down from Montana," said Lacroix. "The Crows, I mean. I figure just passing through. Came upon the camp, caught the Oglalas by surprise. I counted thirty-one bodies. They all stink to high heaven. It must be a week or more since they tangled. From the look of the ground the Crows encircled them."

"How did they keep from being annihilated? How could they get away?"

"I don't know," said Lacroix, looking at Bishop as if he could answer.

Bishop shrugged.

"What are those Indians doing hanging upside down?" Carpenter asked.

"Not doin' much," chimed Bishop.

Others laughed. Carpenter did not. He had been sent out to find prospectors and warn them that "their government strongly suggests they get out of the Black Hills before the end of September." The Sioux were on the warpath. They were not, not yet, but an ounce of prevention... The captain and B Troop had been out four days and had already warned upwards of thirty prospectors. The army had neither the authority nor the inclination to forcibly remove them; Carpenter's orders were to warn them. What they did with his warning was up to them.

"They're not Indians," said Bishop straight-faced. Seemingly trying to atone for his frivolous comment.

"White prospectors," said Lacroix nodding.

"Oh...my...God..." murmured Carpenter. "Ingersoll!"

A burly sergeant with a face as red as a fresh beet and a neck as wrinkled as a turkey's came pounding up, stopping, ripping off a salute.

"Get six men. Cut down those three corpses and bury them properly."

"Yes, sir."

Carpenter studied the dust at his feet and addressed it. "I wonder how many more we'll come across like that. How many more we'll find too late."

"We keep looking, maybe we'll find the boys that did it," said Lacroix. "We could butcher ten or a dozen o' them and hang 'em up the same way. Warnings can work both ways."

Carpenter glared. His tone was reprimanding. "Don't talk nonsense, we're assigned to warn the prospectors not kill Indians. If we did as you suggest it'd be all Sitting Bull and Red Cloud and Crazy Horse would need to light the fuse."

"Which is my point, Captain," said Lacroix evenly. "Showdown is coming, everybody knows that. This wandering around warning the diggers, politely asking them to leave, is shoveling shit against the tide. I'll bet you ten dollars to one not a single one has left, not unless he decides to on his own. They know what the threat is in these hills without us telling them. If they're willing to take their chances . . ." He shrugged.

"You're missing the point, Lacroix," said Carpenter just as evenly, narrowing his eyes to add something akin to a threat. "Whether we end up fighting them or not, we, I mean the fifth, more precisely B Troop, is not going to be the instigator. Colonel Castillo was very clear on that. We have our orders, it's our job to obey them. You know that. Kindly do as I say, and spare us your opinions on the subject."

Lacroix eyed him too long for Carpenter's liking before he mumbled a "sure," spat, and averted his eyes.

The three bodies were cut down and buried, the men assigned to the task working with bandannas tied over their mouths and noses. Two of them could not take the gruesome task, vomiting repeatedly. Sergeant Ingersoll finally replaced them with two others. Meanwhile Carpenter toured the area, inspecting a number of caves with two of his junior officers. They found nothing of either consequence or interest. Both Lacroix and Bishop were sure that a roving party of Crows had attacked the campsite and from all appearances the beleaguered Oglalas had fought back and finally fled. The two scouts were summoned by the captain.

"Any ideas where the Oglalas might have gone?" he asked, looking from one to the other.

Bishop shrugged. Lacroix eyed the captain with a puzzled expression.

"What difference does it make? I mean if we can't bag a few."

"Anton," said Carpenter airily and with obviously forced patience. "Your lust for blood is starting to annoy me. I have a suggestion; if you want to kill Indians so badly, why don't you join up? Enlist with Custer or John Chivington. There's no shortage of Indian haters."

"Or Indian lovers," said Lacroix, smiling, relishing his rejoinder, pleased with himself.

The object of his scorn was not as pleased. His normally pleasant face darkened, tiny storms arose in his eyes, he set his jaw so hard it threatened to dislocate.

"Shut your mouth, half-breed, and keep it shut! We'll be back at the fort in six days. An hour after we get home I want you packed and off the grounds. Your services are no longer needed!"

Bishop's jaw fell as did the jaws of others within earshot. Everyone stood as stiffly as trees, watching.

"You can't fire me. Only the colonel can."

"Take another look at your contract, Mister Blood-and-Thunder. And take a bit of friendly advice. I don't expect everybody on this tour to agree with everything I say or do, but I'll be goddamned if I'll let you or anybody mouth off and insult me to my face. Now get the hell out of my sight before I lose my temper, you insolent scum!"

Lacroix swallowed and backed away. Not out of fear, but out of surprise. Carpenter was an amiable, easy-going man, distressingly unmilitary in many respects, but a good officer, well-liked, respected as a man, dependable, fair, sincere. Not a single man watching had ever seen him raise his voice in such a fashion. It therefore took on greater force and more authority than if he had been a hothead by nature. Seeing the futility of attempting to respond, Lacroix merely nodded, lowered his eyes and started off.

"Hold it!" snarled Carpenter.

The scout stiffened.

"You leave my presence when I dismiss you properly. Not before. Dismissed!"

Twenty minutes later the troop remounted to continue the search-for-and-warn mission.

Raider sat on a flat rock, shoulders sagging, exhausted, and still visibly unnerved by He-Dog's suicide. He had been so shocked and upset when it happened, when he felt He-Dog's hand grip his knife hand and pull the knife down into his throat, Raider had simply let go and backed off. A brave had retrieved the knife and returned it to him. Tried to. He had waved it away, reminding the brave that it belonged to one of his blood brothers. Uttering the word blood brought swirling back the terrible sight of He-Dog murdering himself.

Sitting reflecting on what had happened, he found himself wondering why, among He-Dog's friends, at least one hadn't attacked him. But no one had come near him, not even Crazy Horse. It was over, everyone walked away except two braves who took it upon themselves to remove the body. He had stood transfixed, still in shock, watching them. Then he came out of it and realized that Adrienne was also still standing there, looking as shocked as he did. Saying nothing, only staring. And when he walked away she had followed him up to the rock. Below sprawled the camp. He looked down on it without seeing. She set a comforting hand on his shoulder. He shook it off savagely.

"I'm sorry," she murmured. "Dear, it wasn't your fault."

"Don't call me that! Don't call me anything. Just go away."

"It wasn't. He pulled it into his throat. Everybody saw..."

"I know what he did! I don't need you t' explain. Poor bastard, poor, poor man."

"You don't understand, do you? He wanted to die, to put an end to his suffering, his humiliation. If you hadn't killed him, I mean..."

"Beat it!"

"Please don't be angry with me. I haven't done anything."

"Haven't done anythin'?" He jerked his head up sharply. "God A'mighty, woman, you done everythin'! You caused it all."

She flared angrily. "How can you say such a terrible thing!"

"Never mind, I don't want t' talk 'bout it. Just go away."

"I came to offer you sympathy, understanding. I came as a friend and this is the way you act."

"How the hell do you 'spect me t' act? I saw the way you looked at me while him and me was duelin', with your tongue lickin' your lip, your face all dreamy-eyed."

"Can I help how I feel about you?"

"You don't feel a damn thing. You just wanna get screwed, that's all. Any cock, any time, you don't care beans 'bout the man attached to it, you just want it in you, you slut, bitch!"

"I didn't hear that," she said loftily. "Look, I know you're upset, and perhaps this is the wrong time, but you can't dally, you've got to leave. It's much too dangerous for you here. And please, please don't ask me to go with you. If you ask me a thousand times, my answer will be the same."

He was staring at her. While she was speaking his anger left him and his mind returned to their problem. To discover that the situation had changed radically.

"Wait a minute, stop talkin' an' think a minute. He's dead, your husband. What's keepin' you here? Why stay? There's nothin' for you, not now."

"You're so wrong. You just don't understand, you stubbornly refuse to. I will never leave my people."

"*Your* people! Jesus Christ, gimme a break, willya?"

"Why must you curse every other word? And why can't you at least try to understand? It's really quite simple: I've been given a choice and I've made it and there's no turning back. I don't want to. Accept that, leave here, go back and explain it to Edgar."

"Oh sure..."

"I mean it. Tell him I've made my choice. That I'm sorry, but that's the way it has to be. He's a very practical man, Edgar. He'll accept that it's all over. He'll take it off his shoulders like he does his coat. He'll go straight to a lawyer and draw up the divorce papers. That's his way, everything done according to the rules, everything legal." She was standing before him about three feet away. She leaned over and lowered her voice. "He'll accept it, I guarantee you; why in heaven's name can't you?"

He looked upward at her. She *was* beautiful, he thought, and as resilient and rugged as an Apache. And with a heart of cast iron. She really believed every word out of her mouth. She'd made up her mind and that was that. Still, looking into her eyes, he pondered the situation. Maybe it was time he changed tactics.

"Okay, have it your way."

Her lovely face exploded in a smile. "Wonderful! I knew you'd come around eventually. That I could bring you around. You're a stubborn fellow, but you're not stupid. And you know what they say about women when they've made up their minds."

"Yeah."

He knew all right, and didn't care. It was getting late; he'd finish settling his nerves, then go have a talk with Crazy Horse. Do it right, smart, ask his permission to leave. Tell him he'd given her up as a bad job. He snickered inwardly. Now with He-Dog out of the picture, what if Crazy Horse changed his mind? What if he decided she was excess baggage and wanted her out of there? No, he wouldn't do that, he probably had his eye on her for himself now that she was available.

And what would Black Buffalo Woman think about that?

He'd rest a bit longer, then go and talk to Crazy Horse. He'd leave after dark with or without his blessing. He couldn't imagine he cared enough to stop him. Yes, he'd leave.

And take her with him. Out cold was decidedly preferable to kicking and screaming, waking up the whole tribe.

CHAPTER FIFTEEN

Whether Crazy Horse had designs on He-Dog's widow or not Raider could not decide, but in their brief conversation, although the chief agreed to let Raider ride out, when he suggested that Adrienne go with him all Raider got was a shake of the head. They stood near where Raider had been sitting. Adrienne, confident that she had at last convinced her would-be rescuer that she wasn't interested in being rescued, had walked off. They stood looking off into the clear pale sky; woodpeckers and chickadees sang. In the grass in the distance grouse moved stealthily.

"She has spoken to me. She wishes to stay with us. She has become a friend to Black Buffalo Woman. She does her share of the work, she is no trouble to us."

"She may not be any trouble, but she's damn sure a threat. It's been a couplea weeks now she's been away. Don't be s'prised if the army's out beatin' the bushes lookin' for her. Governor Furnas..."

Crazy Horse's right hand came up, stopping him. "I know, you have already told me. But there is one point you overlook. He-Dog may have abducted her, but she is staying with us because she chooses to. If the soldiers do come and demand we release her, what will she say to them, do you think?"

"Mmmmm, you got a point."

"We do not usually take captives into the tribe, but she came to us."

"Was kidnapped."

"Came to us and wants to stay. I can order her to leave,

to go back with you, but even if she does leave she won't go back to her husband. And won't stay with you. The first chance she gets she will run away from you."

"Maybe, but I'm assigned to bring her back. I'm respons'ble for her."

"You are wrong. She is responsible for herself. She sees you as intruding into her life. She is not a child, she makes her own decisions, and she has decided she wants to stay. Your horse is with our ponies. You may go whenever you please."

"Can I have my forty-five and my little Sharps back?"

"No."

With this he walked off.

"I guess that ends that," growled Raider to himself.

All army officers in the west did not share Captain Willis Carpenter's benevolent attitude toward the Indians. Few did. A tiny percentage of enlisted men did. If they arrived fresh from the east burdened with tolerance for the red man and a pernicious streak of fairness, both speedily left them after their first encounter with the enemy. Indians did not fight fairly, that is sportingly. Their philosophy was simple: When the opportunity presented itself, kill everybody white in sight, regardless of sex, age, or clothing. Settlers died, soldiers died, many hideously, and it was this last that changed the minds of many an enlisted man in regard to the noble savage as characterized by James Fenimore Cooper in his novels which many of them had devoured in their early youths.

Major Philander Stottlemeyer of the Seventh Cavalry did not share Captain Carpenter's humane sentiments toward the Sioux or any other tribe. Stottlemeyer shared Custer's opinion of the hostiles. He despised them and frequently echoed General Philip Sheridan's view expressed while at Fort Cobb in indian territory: "The only good Indians I ever saw were dead."

Unbeknowst to Raider, Crazy Horse, or even Captain Carpenter, that very week the army decided that the very nearly bankrupt Northern Pacific Railroad should be assisted in its endeavors to construct a line along the western edge of the Black Hills. A new fort would have to be built in the Black Hills and Lt. Col. Custer was immediately sent out to locate a suitable site. One day after his arrival, Custer, ever the reckless glorymonger, found a way to win himself national headlines while on his mission. Geologists with his party discovered what more than fifty prospectors already knew. Custer wired back glowing reports of his discovery of gold in the hills which led the press to hail his find as the new Golconda. Within a month hundreds of prospectors would pour in and flood the hills, joining the few already on the scene.

Major Stottlemeyer had no knowledge, nor even a suspicion of this. He, like Captain Carpenter, had been sent to warn the prospectors already digging in the Sioux's sacred hills. Unlike Carpenter, however, Stottlemeyer had no qualms whatsoever about attacking any Indians he came across. Scout Anton Lacroix would have done much better working for the major than for the captain.

It was about an hour to sunset when Stottlemeyer's left flank scout, riding a half mile ahead of the column, sighted the Oglala encampment. He whirled about and galloped back to the column to announce his discovery. Major Stottlemeyer, who looked every inch and curl a West Pointer, which he was—every brass button polished to a gleam, boots shining like sun-splashed mirrors, not a wrinkle in sight, trousers to tunic—greeted the news with a smile so broad it threatened to consume his face.

"How many, Zack?"

"Hard to say, Sir, I mean how many braves. I only saw thirty or forty. Lotsa squaws and kids. Hee hee, they won't put up much of a fight if we hit 'em like a load o' brick, fast and furious, not with their fam'lies out in the open, exposed and all."

"True, true. Captain Kossarian."

An unusually dark-skinned, narrow-faced officer, with

shoulders that sloped sharply down from his thin neck, came dusting up. He reined up, saluting.

"Jess, take a squad and follow Zack here. He's found a Sioux encampment. Be careful as hell now, lest they spot you. Approach with the greatest possible caution; they may have guards posted. They also certainly will, they're mostly women and children."

"May I ask what you intend to do, sir?"

"You may. We'll slaughter the bastards, drape the whole site in blood, women and children, too."

Kossarian reacted, appalled. His face gave silent vent to his feelings.

"You don't approve?" Stottlemeyer asked. "I didn't think you would, but"— he paused and snickered—"lucky for me I don't need your permission, do I now?"

"No sir."

"Get going and remember, the greatest possible caution. And cheer up; we're going to make history. We're going to avenge the Fetterman Massacre, the Bozeman Trail, and every other villainous savage encounter. The Alamo!"

What the Alamo had to do with Indian fighting Kossarian had no idea, but he knew the major, knew the major knew that he lacked the hatred that poured iron into a man's spleen to better fight the hostiles, so he merely nodded, saluted, and rode away to carry out instructions.

Stottlemeyer looked after him, sucked a tooth and shook his head just once.

"That's a good boy, Philander," he murmured. "Good soldier, smart, brave, buttoned up. Just too soft for the job, yessiree. If he doesn't go and get himself killed soon I'll have to think about replacing him."

After talking to Crazy Horse, Raider decided to leave after dark. Well after dark, when everybody except the camp guards were asleep, including Adrienne. He buttoned his conscience up tightly and went to look for her. He found her in his cave. The moment he walked in she began undressing.

"No you don't," he sputtered, gesturing, pushing her away with both hands as if she were about to attack him.

"You're leaving. We may never see each other again. I do like you. I think I may even love you. In spite of all those nasty things you said about my . . . my fondness for . . . you know."

"I know. Man, do I ever . . ."

"What's so terrible about that?"

"The way you go about it; the love o' your life gets chopped off . . ."

"Please!"

She looked horrified. He would have laughed in her face had he not been so annoyed.

"Wounded then; an' you drop him flat. Attack me," he went on.

"Attack? As I recall you were all too willing to have your way with me."

"I like that," he snapped. "Me have *my* way; what about you an' yours? That's what ails you, you know, you're crazy 'bout cock, got no control, an' you don't give a tinker's dam for anybody but yourself."

"That's a vicious thing to say. But I forgive you."

She gave him a charitable smile and resumed undressing. He lunged forward, grabbing her wrists, pulling her hands away from herself.

"Cut it out! I'm not int'rested; I'm not in the mood."

"You don't have to do it to me, I can . . . you know . . ."

"You can't. I don't want it, don't want you. Chrissakes, get it through your head! Get outta here anyway . . ."

"You don't mean that. You enjoy our making love as much as I do, probably more. Please, let's. For old times' sake."

He started to say something, changed his mind, turned, and walked out fuming. Her tinkling laughter followed him. He could feel his cheeks burning. It did nothing to alleviate his disgust with her. But thinking this, he smiled. Would she be surprised when she woke up a half mile from the Nebraska border! She'd be livid! If she made too much of a fuss he'd just have to pop her a second time, put her back to sleep. If necessary he'd tie her wrists and ankles, drape her over her horse and lead her into Collardsville upside down, the object of every tongue waggler's curiosity.

"Dump her on their doorstep, knock on the door an' beat it."

No. That he couldn't do. What he really should do is leave her with Meshach Gatling and go and talk to Edgar. Explain what had happened, leave out the more sordid aspects, definitely omit any allusion to their sex together or hers with He-Dog, say good-bye, and get out of town before Edgar could get over to Gatling's office for the reunion.

He was pushing these thoughts around like sheep blocking the road when a shout went up close by. He raised his head and gasped. A blue column was spilling down the mountainside from the northeast; a cavalry troop, the officer in command riding point, his saber high, catching a ray of the setting sun. Gaining level ground, the troopers spread left and right intending, it appeared, to surround the campsite. Suddenly they vanished into the trees, but he could still hear them. Everybody in camp heard them. The braves hurried to get their weapons, the squaws and children ran for the caves, the old people hobbled after them. The battle was on.

Raider, meanwhile, watched in awe, unable to believe his eyes. Lead began flying. The braves returned fire with their meager supply of rifles. About fifty yards across the way Raider spied Crazy Horse firing the .22 Sharps. Another man was two-handing his confiscated Peacemaker, while he was unarmed, having rejected the dueling knife offered him by the brave. The Indians hadn't even left him his penknife. On the spot he decided there was only one thing to do: Get out now; forget his horse, he'd never reach the stake site far over on the other side, not without catching a stray shot. Run for it, get through the defenders who hopefully would be too busy to worry about him, get through the line of bluecoats, all without a scratch.

He'd have to leave her. He glanced back at the cave. She had come to the entrance and was standing with one hand on the wall, her beautiful face masked with astonishment.

He'd have to leave her, but she'd be all right. He'd explain to the troopers what it was all about, what he was doing in an Oglala camp, tell them about her, and draft them to help him rescue her. From the look of things at the moment, the troopers would make short work of the savages. Again he looked over at Crazy Horse, crouching, continuing to fight back with the .22. In effect his efforts served to symbolize the battle as a whole: A toy pistol pitted against Spencers, Navy Colts, and sabers. But even as Raider looked toward him, Crazy Horse began backing away, calling to the men closest to him.

"He'll get out, take all he can with him." Raider thought aloud.

And fleeing this site promised a good deal easier than getting away from the last one, even with the aid of Mother Nature's rock carving. Unlike the previous camp, this one was crowded with trees and away from the edge of it they were even thicker. The troopers were using trees for cover as were the defenders.

Still, he didn't particularly care what stroke of tactical genius Crazy Horse intended to employ. Only one thing was important: get out and now. He started forward. She called to him.

"No, don't go . . ."

He ignored her, not even turning to look back. Again she called, her voice shrill, clearly audible over the sound of gunfire. In seconds he reached the nearest trees and began dodging from one to the next, confident now that the Indians wouldn't shoot him. Too few guns and not the slightest interest. Still he ran zigzagging and ducking as low as he could without losing sight of the trees immediately in front of him. He passed a corporal down on one knee, his rifle balanced on the other. He paused in his shooting to look up at him questioningly.

"What the hell . . . Where'd you come from?"

Raider was ten feet past him before the boy finished his question. He didn't bother to respond, didn't look back. He ran and ran and ran until his feet turned to lead, his legs to cast iron pipes, his lungs gave out, and down he went, flat on his face.

CHAPTER SIXTEEN

As Raider had expected, Crazy Horse and his followers had run off.

"I've sent twenty men after them under Lieutenant Borzage, my best junior officer," Major Stottlemeyer explained. "Zack Ayres went along; best Indian scout in the whole Department of Dakota. They'll catch up. How come you're so eager to?"

He was studying Raider with a look that wasn't getting him an answer to his question, but was making Raider extremely uncomfortable. He hesitated to say anything about Adrienne Dubois. Edgar had shied away from alerting the army for a good reason. There *are* jobs in this world that don't call for two hundred men dressed in blue. It was probably the only intelligent contribution Edgar had made to the whole mess. Raider read Stottlemeyer as a minor version of Custer; too eager for the headlines rescuing Adrienne would bring him to settle for anything but a massacre in the attempt.

"Me and Crazy Horse got unfinished bus'ness," Raider lied.

"You've actually been with them for two whole weeks and lived to tell of it? And not a scratch on you, far as I can see. What have you been doing, trading them whiskey? You one of them?"

"I already tolja', I'm a Pinkerton oper'tive assigned to ... I can't tell you, we're not supposed to talk about our cases. Agency rule. Here for Chrissakes ..."

He got his wallet out and showed his I.D. card.

114

"What in hell is a Pinkerton doing in the Black Hills?" Stottlemeyer asked.

"I just finished tellin' you!"

"You haven't told me a blessed thing! Don't get your feathers up."

"I'm sorry..."

"Boy, you sure got some hair-trigger temper. You always so grouchy?"

"What would you be? Half an hour ago I was standin' twenty feet from 'im. Now he's miles away an' gettin' farther every shake. I gotta get goin'. Catch up with your scout an' your shavetail an' the rest. I need a gun an' a horse."

"We lost six men, preliminary count," said the major grimly. "I guess we can spare one of each."

"I want a mare."

"Hey, don't go getting choosy. You'll take what you get."

Raider made a resentful sound deep in his throat, but resisted putting his feelings into words. He'd catch up with Adrienne again. They'd fled to the north; they probably wouldn't go too far, not burdened with the old and the very young and the women the way they were. Just far enough to shake their pursuers. Stottlemeyer, Mr. Spit-and-Polish, had great good confidence in his scout and his shavetail.

Raider laughed to himself; he'd bet on Crazy Horse.

The horse given him was a gelding, big and strong-muscled, surprisingly durable, especially on steep grades. Raider continued not to worry about catching up with the tribe. What happened when he managed to was another matter. He was not about to ride boldly into camp. Instead he'd locate it, sneak up close enough to familiarize himself with the setup, determine, if possible, where she was bedding down, wait till the darkest hour of the night, move on in, and bring her out.

"You make it sound so easy," he muttered to himself. "That's one o' your biggest friggin' faults, over-conf'dence. Talking a thing through to death, jinxin' the actual doin' for fair. Every time. So shut up."

For some reason he suddenly found himself thinking not of Adrienne, nor Crazy Horse, but somebody out of the past: His old partner Doc Weatherbee.

How would Doc go about getting her out of the camp? Partners working on a case generally did things differently than lone operatives. It sure would be easier if Doc were here. Smartest man he'd ever known, and the gutsiest. To think an Ivy-leaguer, a fingernail-manicured city boy who'd started out not knowing one end of a horse or a gun from the other could turn into such a crackerjack. Best partner any Pinkerton ever had.

The best. One thing he'd come in handy for in this one, he sure knew how to handle women; he could figure their crazy thinking, make sense of it. He'd make sense of her and know instinctively what to say to her, how to talk her into changing her mind.

But Doc wasn't here and never would be again. He rode on, picking up the pace. The woods were so thick it was easy to follow the Oglalas and their pursuers by the broken branches and trampled brush. Presently, after about five miles of woods riding, boughs thrashing both him and the horse, Raider emerged into an open area cluttered with shrubs and beautifully colored with lupines. Far ahead, a third of the way up a steep slope, Raider saw dust and squinting, made out moving blue figures. At the summit dust also rose.

"Thatta boy, Crazy Horse, keep movin'. . ."

He had to hand it to the white Indian, he fought pale eyes, blue soldiers, other tribes, and always wriggled out of it to fight again. And won far more battles than he lost. Had he been white and fifteen years older he'd have led his class at West Point and might even have led the North or the South, supplanting Grant or Robert E. Lee in the recent hostilities.

Spying the dust, realizing it would be at least ten minutes before the lieutenant and his men reached the mountaintop, Raider pulled up sharply, dismounted, and unbuckled the girth of his saddle. Removing it, he tossed it aside. He couldn't stand the regulation cavalry dish pan, no pommel, no room, no comfort; more uncomfortable than a Hussey reaper seat. Felt like it, like steel. Designed by the devil himself. Better to ride bareback.

He remounted and sprinted off. Stottlemeyer would be sure to ask what had happened to his saddle. Even a civilian had no right to throw away army equipment. He'd think of some explanation.

Boy, bareback felt good!

CHAPTER SEVENTEEN

ALLAN PINKERTON CHIEF PINKERTON NATIONAL DETECTIVE AGENCY 191 193 FIFTH AVENUE CHICAGO ILL STOP THIS IS TO INFORM YOU THAT I AM HEREBY SEVERING OUR AGREEMENT STOP IN LIGHT FACT YOU HAVE FAILED TO ACCEDE MY WISHES IN REPLACING RAIDER YOU LEAVE ME NO ALTERNATIVE STOP THE MAN IS INCOMPETENT WILLFUL IRRESPONSIBLE UNCOOPERATIVE IN ALL A PERILOUS THREAT TO MY WIFES WELFARE AND SURVIVAL STOP AM OBLIGED TO ADD THAT YOUR CONDUCT IN THIS SORRY AFFAIR AND YOUR CAVALIER RESPONSE TO MY REQUEST IN THAT YOU SEE FIT TO DELIBERATELY PLACE LOYALTY TO YOUR MAN OVER THE SAFETY OF MY POOR WIFE IS OUTRAGEOUS

                                                E DEBOIS

HARMON DUBOIS KANSAS FARMERS MERCHANTS BANK KANSAS CITY KANSAS STOP HAVE JUST DISPATCHED WIRE TO PINKERTON DISSOLVING OUR AGREEMENT STOP OPERATIVE HE ASSIGNED TO TRACK DOWN AND RESCUE ADRIENNE FAILED COMPLETELY LEAVING ME NO ALTERNATIVE BUT TO DISCHARGE AGENCY STOP INTEND TO HIRE THREE OR FOUR MEN LOCALLY TO ATTEMPT RESCUE STOP LET HER CONTINUE TO HAVE YOURS AND MOTHERS PRAYERS STOP REALIZE PINKERTON YOUR OLD AND DEAR FRIEND AND HESITATE TO CRITICIZE HIS JUDGMENT BUT MUST HOLD HIM PERSONALLY RESPONSIBLE FOR FAILING TO HOLD UP AGENCYS END IN THIS GRIEVOUS SITUATION

STOP GOD WILLING IT IS STILL NOT TOO LATE TO SAVE
MY DARLING STOP LOVE TO MOTHER

    E

HARMON DUBOIS KANSAS FARMERS MERCHANTS
BANK KANSAS CITY KANSAS STOP IN HAND TELEGRAM
FROM EDGAR DISCHARGING US FOR REASONS AM SURE
HE HAS ALREADY MADE PLAIN TO YOU STOP IN CONSIDERATION OUR FRIENDSHIP AND AGENCYS REPUTATION FEEL OBLIGED TO EXPLAIN STOP ASSIGNED BEST
AVAILABLE MAN TO CASE STOP DISAGREEMENT BETWEEN HIM AND EDGAR INFURIATED EDGAR STOP
NEVERTHELESS OPERATIVE ASSIGNED THE BEST
CHOICE I COULD HAVE MADE AND WOULD MAKE SAME
AGAIN IF CALLED UPON TO STOP SUCCESSFUL BUSINESS PARTNERS OFTEN DESPISE EACH OTHER

    A P

EDGAR DUBOIS COLLARDSVILLE NEBRASKA STOP
YOUR TELEGRAM RECEIVED STOP SUGGEST YOU REREAD OUR STANDARD AGREEMENT STOP ATTENTION
PARAGRAPH NINE PAGE THREE STOP QUOTE IN EVENT
OPERATIVE ASSIGNED CASE IS REQUIRED TO REMOVE
SELF TO WILDERNESS DESERT ANY AREA IN PURSUIT
HIS DUTIES RENDERING COMMUNICATION IMPOSSIBLE
AND CLIENT ELECTS TO DISSOLVE THIS AGREEMENT
HE AGREES TO POSTPONE SAID DISSOLUTION UNTIL OPERATIVE CAN BE INFORMED AND ABLE TO CONFIRM
SAID INTELLIGENCE STOP AM PRESENTLY READING
YOUR SIGNATURE ON OUR COPY OF AGREEMENT CONCURRING WITH THIS STOP APPRECIATE YOUR UNDERSTANDING OF NECESSITY OF THIS STIPULATION STOP
DO NOT LOSE HEART RAIDER WILL RESCUE HER

    A P

ALLAN PINKERTON CHIEF PINKERTON NATIONAL DETECTIVE AGENCY 191 193 FIFTH AVENUE CHICAGO ILL
STOP YOUR TELEGRAM RECEIVED STOP EXPLANATION
APPRECIATED STOP WOULD ONLY REMIND YOU THAT

EDGAR IS UNDER GREAT STRAIN AND UNDER CIRCUMSTANCES HIS IMPULSIVENESS MUST BE FORGIVEN STOP LEAVE IT TO ME TO REASSURE HIM AND URGE PATIENCE FORTITUDE AND CONFIDENCE IN YOUR MAN

H

EDGAR DUBOIS COLLARDSVILLE NEBRASKA STOP CALM DOWN SON YOU ARE DEALING WITH WORLDS FOREMOST DETECTIVE AGENCY STOP AP IS A MASTER AT HIS CRAFT STOP REST ASSURED MAN HE HAND PICKED TO FIND ADRIENNE TOP NOTCH STOP PRAY SON STOP MOTHER SENDS LOVE

H

ALLAN PINKERTON CHIEF PINKERTON NATIONAL DETECTIVE AGENCY 191 193 FIFTH AVENUE CHICAGO ILL STOP HAVE REREAD AGREEMENT AS YOU SUGGESTED STOP MY LAWYER INFORMS ME IT IS NOT BINDING STOP NOT WORTH PAPER IT IS WRITTEN ON STOP AGENCY DISCHARGED DISCHARGED DISCHARGED THIS DATE STOP DO NOT CONTACT ME FURTHER

E

"Close the door like a good chap, would you?" said Edgar, half rising from behind his desk. "And please take chairs."

The four men invited into his office did not look like loan applicants. Nor even like people with checking or savings accounts. They looked like what they were, four rugged, earthy types who worked as infrequently as was necessary and loafed and spreed and brawled the remainder of the time. Their pasts were as shady as their stubbled cheeks and chins, they had seen the inside of Meshach Gatling's cells, they had dallied in small crime and were suspected of big crime. They were perfect in every respect for the assignment Edgar was about to give them. And not one reacted to his jaw protector, he was pleased to see.

Two were the Halliburton brothers, Edgar (coincidentally) and Ira-Vance. They were part-time sugar beet farmers and full-time troublemakers, rowdies who rarely came into town to do anything other than raise hell. Ira-Vance was four years his brother's junior, an ugly, obnoxious illiterate, gifted with an astonishingly accurate shooting eye and cursed with a speech impediment and the shrill voice of a schoolgirl. Brother Edgar had the looks in the family, and the conceit, and a gift of gab that turned empty women's heads and had already earned him three accusations of rape, none of which the circuit riding judge was able to make stick.

The third member of the group was Hannibal McCorkle, a good-natured, harmless, easily-led youngster who idolized Edgar Halliburton and probably would have strolled barefoot into hell if Edgar off-handedly suggested it. Edgar Dubois' fourth visitor was Roger Wizlowski, who was about 28, tall, lean, and disagreeable, a man who was seemingly making a career out of annoying Sheriff Gatling. His specialty was drinking himself rigid and turning his filthy mouth loose in the presence of ladies. But, like Ira-Vance, he could shoot. And ride and fight and kill (if the chance presented itself and he thought he could get away with it).

Edgar got a bottle and three glasses out of the bottom drawer of his desk.

"Afraid I've got only three glasses," he said apologetically.

"We don't need no glasses," averred his namesake. "Give 'er here."

Edgar Halliburton did not wait to be given the bottle; he stood up and practically snatched it from the banker's grasp. And read the label.

"Farquharson's Scotch Whisky, product o' Scotland." He whistled admiringly, upended the bottle and downed a triple slug. "Man, that's tasty, sweet as honey an' bites like a bulldog."

"Give me thome," lisped his brother and also declined to wait, jumping up and grabbing the bottle. His brother snatched it back. Ira-Vance grabbed it a second time. Suddenly they were fighting over it. The other two separated them, everyone sat down, Dubois sighed inwardly, eyed the ceiling, watched them pass the rapidly emptying bottle from hand to hand and politely asked for their full attention.

He told them what had happened from the outset. Everyone in Collardsville and for miles around knew about the abduction but so much conjecture, so many rumors swirled about the truth Edgar was constrained to correct misunderstandings from all four of his listeners after he was done recounting the events. It did not take him long to tell his story. All he really knew was what Wesley Frazier had told him, but it could be logically assumed that Adrienne's abductors had headed for the Black Hills after they'd taken her.

"We'll find her, Mister Dubois," said Wizlowski jauntily. "All we gotta do is find them red bastards and we'll find her, right?"

This seemed so abundantly obvious to Edgar, so unnecessary to put into words, he couldn't think of a response.

"There's just one thing you boys have to know," he said. "I hired the Pinkertons to find her."

"What the hell you need with us then!" flared his namesake irritably.

"Please. I hired them, I fired them. They're completely out of the picture. Only one thing, the man the agency assigned is still out in the field; in the Black Hills, probably. There's no way to get in touch with him. I can't contact him to tell him he's off the case. He doesn't know. He's still working on finding her."

"What if he does?" asked Wizlowski. "He maybe already has."

"He hasn't," responded Edgar. "Trust me. Bumbling idiot couldn't find his face in the mirror."

"Couldn' find his ath with hith right hand on the john!" shrilled Ira-Vance and cackled uproariously.

Edgar winced. What was going on in the privacy of his office was nobody's business outside, only Ira-Vance seemed determined to make it everybody's.

"Can we keep it down?" asked Edgar politely. "If you

boys can track those savages down and rescue her unscathed, and without the Pinkerton getting in your way, bring her back here in good health, as good as can be expected, considering she's already been out there nearly two weeks... Damn, when I think of all the hideous things those animals must have done to her, it sickens me. Forgive me; sometimes it just gets to me. As I was saying, you boys bring her back safely and you'll be handsomely rewarded. Handsomely."

"How handsome is that?" asked his namesake.

"Five hundred dollars apiece."

All whistled, impressed; two of them clapped. Edgar Halliburton did not react. He sat staring at the man with the leather-encased jaw.

"That ain't fair. I'm the leader. I should get more."

"You'll get seven fifty. But only if she's unharmed. If, God forgive me, the worst happens..."

"If they rape her to death," interposed Wizlowski.

"If they kill her," Edgar corrected him, "you'll be paid two hundred dollars for your efforts."

"Fair enough," said Wizlowski.

The elder Halliburton whirled on him angrily.

"I'm supposed to say that Roger Wiz, I'm leader!" He turned back to Edgar, his expression softening. "I say it: fair 'nough."

Edgar leaned back in his chair, stretching his legs under the desk out of sight, tenting his fingers and looking from face to face.

"Done. When will you leave?"

"Right awa..."

Wizlowski stopped short and looked toward Edgar Halliburton. The king nodded, granting permission to speak. Wizlowski lost his chance to. Ira-Vance butted in.

"Right away!" he burst brightly.

The bottle was empty, the agreement consummated, the amount of the reward fixed. The four left, leaving their chairs in disarray and their employer scowling.

"Disgusting trash. Revolting!"

He shuddered as if their presence were a cloak that he

wanted to throw off. But then he smiled and congratulated himself. He couldn't have picked four men better suited to the job. They were perfect: Hard-bitten Indian haters, greedy for money, resourceful, capable, totally immoral. They'd rescue her. A slender dart of worry pierced his thoughts. The older Halliburton had a reputation for womanizing women against their will. He hesitated to call it rape. Still, he'd never been convicted and wouldn't dare touch Adrienne, helpless as she was. If he even so much as laid his hand on her arm he'd forfeit every cent of his reward. He knew that.

Edgar crinkled his nose at the stink of body odor they left in the air, then he ran a hand over his leather covered jaw. Not one of them had commented on it; no snickering, no snide remarks behind their hands, although when they'd first sat down they had stared.

"Stupid clods."

Again he smiled as a pleasing thought came to mind. It was possible they'd not only rescue her, but eliminate Raider, providing he was with her. That was doubtful, but if he were they'd see him as competition and a threat to their money, and likely wouldn't hesitate to do him in. Sheriff Gatling might wonder what had happened to him after it was all over, wonder why he seemed to vanish into the air, but knowing Meshach, his curiosity wouldn't be great enough to pry him out of his chair and into an investigation.

"On the other hand, Raider probably hasn't even located her yet. He's probably out wandering around forty miles from their camp."

There was a third possibility. Maybe her kidnappers had caught up with Raider and scalped him, killed him.

"Wouldn't that be nice!"

To never have to lay eyes on the drunken scoundrel again. And have the last laugh with that insufferable Allan Pinkerton!

CHAPTER EIGHTEEN

Raider caught up with Lieutenant Borzage, Zack Ayres, the scout, and the twenty men about four miles from where he'd disposed of the saddle. He sighted them resting at the top of the mountain. Ascending it, he marveled at the gelding's seemingly inexhaustible strength. It was rare to find a horse with such stamina.

"You're a U.S. of A. army horse; I'm gonna call you Gen'ral Miles after the genuine article. Gen'ral 'cause you're army and Miles on accounta you sure can cover 'em."

The detachment at the summit saw him following and waited for him. General Miles came scrambling up. Raider hadn't met Borzage, but when Major Stottlemeyer mentioned his name he'd remembered it. Borzage was a troubled-looking individual, no more than 26 or 27, with a face like a badger, wedge-shaped, with soulful brown eyes and an almost total absence of chin. Ayres appeared to be thirty years olders than Borzage, although he was probably only in his late thirties. He was a dried up little man with one slightly crossed eye and a cheek packed as hard as a doorknob with cut plug. He was dressed like a tramp. Raider returned both men's greetings and swept the horizon with a quick glance; there was no sign of the Oglalas, not a wisp of dust above the distant trees. He showed Borzage his I.D. and recounted his conversation with the major.

"How come you're stopping?" he asked.

Borzage shook his head. He looked like a nice young fellow to Raider, not a professional soldier, just a hired hand doing his job and, from his expression, not exactly reveling in it at the moment. The lieutenant answered the question with a single shake of his head. His men had gotten down and were attending to their mounts. All the horses were lathered with sweat and blowing hard. Two or three looked to be on the brink of collapse.

"This is as far as we go," Borzage said. "We've ridden our poor horses into the ground; they'll never make the next mountain. The major's had us out looking for prospectors fourteen hours a day. I tried to tell him we'll wind up killing the horses, pushing 'em so hard, but he doesn't listen. Never does. He thinks Colonal Custer's God and can do no wrong, and when he orders his men to ride their horses into the ground, it makes sense. Anything Custer does Philander has to. Hero worship. Like a little kid. I was hoping after that set-to back there we'd get at least a couple hours to catch our breaths, but hell no. Well, this is as far as we go; we can't keep on even if we wanted. We'll rest a couple hours and head on back."

Raider had not asked for such a lengthy explanation, didn't feel entitled to it, but he listened without interruption, deciding that the lieutenant just wanted to get it off his chest. And quiet his conscience.

Raider shrugged. "Stottlemeyer's not gonna be too pleased."

"Fuck Philander," snapped Borzage. "I don't give two hoots. I've got one foot out the door of this man's army and the other on a patch of ice. I've had my fill of Indians, dust, the winters, the heat, the bugs, snakes, chicken-shit orders, and dress parade. I'm going home to San Jose and raise plums and green grapes, play my zither, marry my girl, and have sixteen kids."

"Good for you, how many years you put in?"

"Too many. Five next month. You going on?"

"I have to."

Again Raider looked off toward the next mountain.

"Maybe nobody's tolja," interposed Ayres, "but that's Crazy Horse up ahead." He spat, relieving the pressure in his cheek. "You'd best not tangle yourself up with him."

"Him and me got unfinished bus'ness," said Raider evenly.

Ayres looked surprised. "A Pink and a Sioux chief?"

"Pers'nal unfinished bus'ness."

Borzage grinned. "And you can mind your own business, Zachary, right, Mr. Raider? Well, *vaya con dios*."

Ayres nodded and grinned toothlessly. "Watch your hind end and keep your head down. And easy on your horse, it's got to be as tired as ours be."

Raider patted the gelding's neck. It swished its tail appreciatively.

"You're not tired, are you, Gen'ral? This boy's got leg power like you wouldn't believe, don'cha, pardner?"

The lieutenant looked down the slope and away into the thick pines marching north. "You may not have far to go. It's getting dark fast. Another ten minutes you won't be able to see your horse's head. Nor will they. My guess is they'll be stopping soon."

"Already have," said Ayres and spat again. "The hell with 'em."

With which he sat down on the ground, pulled off his boots and began massaging his feet.

"So long," said Raider to Borzage. "Tell Stottlemeyer I'll take good care o' his horse."

"What happened to your saddle?"

"Fell off."

With this Raider rode away, avoiding any necessity for further explanation. Without turning to look back he could see both their puzzled expressions. He chuckled.

Crazy Horse ordered his followers to halt and make camp in the shadow of a hill about a half hour's ride south of Harney Peak. Every pony had been double ridden and was too exhausted to go on. Two braves who had been sent back to check on their pursuers returned with word that the blue soldiers had given up the chase. Adrienne, who had shared her pony's back with two small children given her by Black Buffalo Woman, gave them back and went to look for Crazy Horse.

She found him talking to four braves. She waited patiently for them to finish their conversation and when they did and Crazy Horse started to walk over and rejoin Black Buffalo Woman, Adrienne caught up with him. When he turned to look at her she immediately saw that his eyes were not friendly. Why weren't they? she wondered. She hadn't done anything to offend him; they had not even seen each other since the flight began. She decided it wasn't anything she'd done, merely that she was still hanging around. Perhaps, she thought, Crazy Horse saw no reason for her to do so with He-Dog dead and the Pinkerton gone. He certainly wasn't interested in her and until she found another protector she was just excess baggage.

Crazy Horse wasn't attracted to her not because he didn't like women, not because she wasn't attractive, but because, unlike He-Dog, he was too proud to give himself to such an alliance. It would, mused Adrienne, diminish him in the eyes of his followers. That would never do, Caesar must never look less than Caesar.

He gave her a minute.

"I just wanted you to know," she began haltingly, avoiding his eyes, "I want to stay with you if you'll let me. I want to be one of you; I feel I belong with you."

"Do you?" It seemed to amuse him; he made a half-hearted effort to conceal a smirk.

"I'm being serious."

He shrugged. "If your heart tells you that you do, then you do. Or..." He paused and narrowed his eyes. They glinted in the moonlight and seemed to see into her brain. "Is it that you don't feel you belong with your own people?"

She stiffened, her self-consciousness fleeing, displaced by annoyance.

"I belong where I want to be. I am my own master. But see here, I do want to stay. Really. I'll do anything asked of me, any work. I can help with the children, with the cooking; I can help treat the wounded. I was a nurse's aide once back East. I can stand the sight of blood."

"Good. So far you've seen little compared with what you're going to see. If you do stay."

"Will you fight the army? Will you ally with other tribes and fight? I think you must, or be annihilated. You must fight for your rights, for your land. It *is* your land, these hills, they have no right to be here; when they attacked back there they were breaking their own law. Isn't that despicable?"

His face said he didn't understand the word. What he did understand, however, was her loyalty and enthusiasm. Both came from her heart, both were genuine. He touched her arm in a friendly gesture. She tingled at his touch. She nearly cried out it lifted her so.

"You can stay with us, but no one is forcing you to...."

"I know, I know..."

"It will not be easy, it will be dangerous, and there will be no end to it. *In* the end..."

He shrugged as if to invite her imagination to fill in the blank. This she did not do; she barely heard his warning so delighted was she that he had touched her arm, transported by this simple friendly gesture.

Edgar Dubois's four hired guns rode north toward the border of the Black Hills beyond. With them they brought two jugs of the Halliburton brothers' corn squeezings. Young Hannibal McCorkle had downed his share of Dubois's whiskey in the banker's office, but confessed to having no taste for Edgar Halliburton's corn liquor.

"I'm sorry, Edgar, but that stuff tastes like rotten sheep dip."

Edgar swigged, passed the bottle to Roger Wizlowski, leered, and wiped the liquor from his chin with his sleeve.

"You got to grow up to it, boy; your taster ain't devel'ped yet. It's a man's drink."

Hannibal scowled. "You sayin' I ain't a man?"

"Man has a man's taste, boy has a boy's."

Wizlowski, somewhat more intelligent and perceptive than his companions, could see an argument budding. He quickly changed the subject to one of interest to all that happily invited no difference of opinion.

"Five hundred dollars... Woowee!" he burst. "That's more money than I ever saw my whole life!"

"I seen it," said Edgar smugly. "Seen thousands in the bank vault when they had the door wide open. Stacks and stacks o' greenbacks."

Wizlowski laughed. "Who's talking about money in the bank? I'm talking money in your pocket. Five hundred green dollars, wow!"

"We firtht gotta find the woman," interposed Ira-Vance.

"Find them that took her and we find her," said Edgar. "Shouldn't be too hard, not like lookin' for a needle in a haystack."

"What about that Pinkerton Mr. Dubois told us about?" Wizlowski asked. "What if he's already saved her?"

"Maybe he has, maybe not." Edgar picked up the pace, the others following suit. "But he sure ain't brought her back yet. And they gotta come back down this road. It's the only road north outta Collardsville. And if they do..."

"We thtop 'em and take her away from him," interrupted Ira-Vance. "Right, Ed?"

"You betcha."

"How we supposed to do that?" Wizlowski asked. "What if he doesn't want to give her up? He won't want to."

"You s'prise me, Roger, you dis'point me. Man it'll be us four against one; whatta we care what he wants? If he gives us any fuss, we'll just shoo him away. If he really gives us trouble, I'll put one in his face."

"Right in front o' her?" Wizlowski persisted.

"He'th right, Ed," said Ira-Vance. "You cain't shoot him in fronta her, she'll be a witneth."

Edgar scowled and slowed his horse. He stopped, they stopped. Edgar got down. They were about a mile from the Dakota border. They had been riding for nearly an hour. The sun had climbed halfway to its zenith in the radiant sky. Edgar removed his hat and swiped his brow with his forearm. The others also dismounted. Annoyance overspread Edgar's good looks.

"She will be," repeated his brother.

Edgar whirled on him. "You think I'm stupid, you lispin' jackass? You think I don't know that? Let me tell you all something 'fore we go one step further." He tapped his temple. "This here brain has figured out 'zactly how we handle that Pinkerton. We don't kill him in fronta the woman, I never said we would. Did I, Roger?"

"Well . . ."

"I didn't! What we do if we come upon the two of 'em together is stop and interduce ourselves as polite as the parson, and I'll take the woman to one side and tell her what we're doin' there, how her husban' hired us special, that we're 'sponsible for her and suchlike. I'll walk her outta sight o' you all and him and Ira-Vance, and then you'll plug him."

"Can I? Am I to be the one?"

Hannibal also brightened. Roger did not.

"What's the matter, Roger?" Edgar asked pointedly.

"I don't like it, I think it stinks."

Edgar bristled indignantly. "Can you think of a better way to get rid o' him?"

"Anybody with half a brain could," responded Wizlowski evenly. "Killing him out of sight of her doesn't do anything; she'll still know we killed him in cold blood. And she'll know why: so we can be sure we'll get our money. It's gotta be smarter than that. Dubois said he fired him, only couldn't get in touch with him to tell him so."

"What you're saying is we tell him," said Edgar.

"Right. It's a true fact. If he goes running back to Mr. Dubois, which he's bound to, *he'll* back it up."

"Only one thing," said Edgar. "What if the Pinkerton doesn't believe us? What if she doesn't?"

Wizlowski gave him the most patronizing look he could muster, wondering as he did, what he was doing out here with such as these. Then he remembered the money.

"I'm sure we can think up something better 'n gunnin' him down in cold blood," he said.

"You work out somethin'," Edgar snapped. "You find fault with what I think up, go 'head and think up somethin' better. Go 'head, do it, do it!"

"He'th right about that," lisped Ira-Vance in a singsong gloating tone.

"Who asked you?" snarled Wizlowski. "Pass the jug, dammit!"

All Raider could see of the Oglalas down the far side of the second mountain were their cook fires when the darkness settled in. He hobbled General Miles on a grassy patch and ate a cold supper of beans, biscuits, and water from his canteen rendered tepid by the broiling sun, hesitating to light a fire for fear some sharp-eyed brave would see the smoke and come and investigate.

He could do nothing tonight. He would bed down here where the trees were particularly dense, sleep, get up with the sun and spend the day reconnoitering the new campsite. He wished he'd been able to hang onto the opera glasses, but they had gone the way of the Sharps, his Peacemaker and junk jewelry, likely never to be seen again.

Adrienne would be up early and out with the others, he'd see her, get a fix on where she was sleeping and snatch her the following night. He'd try to pull it off without being spotted coming or going. He wondered what Crazy Horse would say if he caught him? He wouldn't be exactly surprised to see him. Would Crazy Horse let him take her? She'd be sure to put up a squawk. Crazy Horse would probably let her have her way and send him packing with a warning not to show up a third time.

He would have all the next day to plan his move on her, plenty of time to figure out the best way possible to go about it. They'd made a good selection for a campsite; the trees were as dense here as anywhere in the Hills. But there'd been nothing wrong with the first two locations. The Crows had driven them away from one, the army from the other.

"Who's next?"

He lay under a tree about twenty feet from where he'd

hobbled his horse. He kept the gun Stottlemeyer had given him cocked and ready, just in case a four-legged something with teeth, claws, and a nasty disposition was lurking about. He did not fall asleep right away. He lay thinking—not about the situation and the impending showdown, if indeed there was to be a showdown—but of all things, Amory Wiggins, his mule Eleanor, his flea-bitten chestnut stallion Harold. By now the old man had undoubtedly picked up his supplies, his liquor for the winter, and had returned to the Hills. Raider had come to like him in spite of his redolence. He worried about him. The major and his men were riding around warning prospectors to get out before the Indians took to the warpath. Indeed, they'd already started with the three men Crazy Horse's followers had caught and strung up and stoned to death. Would Amory die upside down, red as a tomato from his heels to his head, stinking for the last time? He'd survived in strange places on his own for a long time, but in this life, in these times, in this place, disaster could strike like lightning.

General Miles whinnied.

"Go t' sleep, Gen'ral, there's nothin' we can do for the old goat."

CHAPTER NINETEEN

It began to rain in the middle of the night. By morning it was a deluge. All morning long Raider waited for it to let up enough to permit him to see through it and observe the Oglalas' campsite. It finally abated just before noon. Around one the sun came out, setting the hilly green landscape gleaming. The trees dripped in chorus. Raider laid his shirt and pants on a rock to dry and crept in his underwear out to the end of a ledge from where he could look down upon the Indians. There were no caves here that he could see and the Indians were not putting up wickiups, which suggested that they would probably be moving on soon. He wondered where and considered the possible destinations. Likeliest was west to the Wyoming border and across the Great Plains, across the Belle Fourche River to the Powder River country.

If I don't get her out o' there t'night, he thought, *I'll haveta follow 'em, maybe all the way.*

Thinking further about it, as he lay on the ledge, it struck him that at that very moment he was no better off than when the hunting party brought him into the first camp and he caught sight of her. Actually worse off, having already had his chance and blown it, thereby losing the element of surprise.

He reconnoitered all afternoon. Activity in the camp included preparations for moving out; Crazy Horse sent ten men north, Raider guessed to steal horses to replace those lost and left behind in the first two encounters, and Adrienne appeared in the company of a brave Raider did not recognize, but at that distance he could not make out anyone's features, and was only able to identify Adrienne by her fair skin. Any grief she might have felt for He-Dog appeared to have vanished. She clung to her new man's arm so it looked embarrassing, only evidently not to either of them. He'd probably find them locked in each other's arms when he went in to get her that night. He hoped he'd at least find them asleep.

Fortunately, it clouded over just before sunset; the sky took on a sullen look, the bright blue giving way to bruise-grey and when darkness arrived neither moon nor stars were visible. After night had settled upon the land like a down comforter on a bed Raider waited six more hours before starting out, estimating each hour singly and joining the last one to the others in turn. Earlier, even before the sun began to sink below the horizon, he had deserted his ledge and circled the camp, looking for the Oglalas' corral, but he was unable to find it, sighting only a few scattered ponies. The detachment that had ridden out before it stopped raining had not returned, but they could at any time, and perhaps that was all Crazy Horse was waiting for before he gave the order to move out.

Raider estimated the time at about 3 A.M. when he decided to make his move. He had pinpointed where Adrienne and her new lover were bedded down, a spot to the east about twenty yards from the main camp, affording them relative privacy. Raider circled around to that side and started in. It was darker than he had anticipated and he made his way through the trees almost like a blind man, trying his utmost to keep his direction. Luck was with him: He spotted their dying fire about a hundred feet ahead and made straight for it. He heard them before he saw them; they were making love and plainly enjoying it. It would have been embarrassing had it not been such a critical phase in the "rescue."

Kidnappin's more like it, he thought to himself as he approached. *That's sure as hell what she's gonna call it.*

Her lover was on top of her, pumping away vigorously. Her legs locked around his, she dug her nails into his broad back and attacked his face with her mouth, biting, sucking, squealing, panting horsely, and demanding he rip her, rip her...

Raider moved up to them from below their feet, straddling their legs and cold-cocking the brave with the butt of his Colt. The Indian sighed as he lost consciousness. Raider was pulling him off her when she realized what had happened. She started to scream; he hit her with his fist to shut her up, cursing as he did, stiffening, wondering if anyone nearby was awake and heard. She lay as limp as a rag doll. He rolled her lover, erection and all, off her onto his back, picked her up and slung her over his shoulder. Then lay her back down. She was naked. He couldn't take her without something to cover her. He fumbled about in the darkness and, after what seemed a half hour, found her clothes. He dressed her. He had gotten on her mocassins and was about to pick her up when the brave groaned and stirred. And to Raider's astonishment jumped up roaring. He, too, was naked. He threw himself at Raider, seizing him by the throat. He was bigger, stronger than He-Dog. Raider felt like a pair of wide-blade cutting nippers had hold of him. He drove his fists straight upward between the brave's forearms, breaking his grip, gasping, staggering back to catch his breath. His windpipe felt shattered, squeezed together like a cardboard tube in the hand of a child. The brave lunged forward to get hold a second time. Raider stepped aside and turned, at the same time sticking his leg out, tripping him in a heap. His throat on fire, pain exploding, he threw himself down on the brave, cursing. His anger and haste ill served him. He suddenly found himself in a wrestling match when he might better have stayed on his feet and hit the brave a second time with the Colt. Raider was thinking this as the brave locked his arms about Raider's chest from behind. While driving one knee into the ground he tried to lift Raider up to bear hug his lungs flat. Raider lifted his leg and heeled him as hard as he could in the instep. The brave howled and let him loose; Raider fumbled out his gun and leveled it as his chest.

"Hold it, goddamnit!"

On he came, Raider stepped back, brought up the gun

and smashed his temple with the barrel, dropping him. He retrieved Adrienne and, draping her over his shoulder, he stepped over her prostrate lover, and started off the way he'd come. He had not taken ten steps before a figure loomed up before him and a familiar voice spoke.

"Stop. Put her down."

"Not a chance. Just lemme go, lemme take her. Let us both get outta your hair. You got troubles 'nough without us."

At that moment the overcast parted, revealing the full moon. Its light silvered the blade of the knife in Crazy Horse's rising hand. In simultaneous motion Raider dropped her and kicked, catching Crazy Horse full in the shin, setting him hopping and howling. Then he smashed him in the side of the jaw with his fist, silencing him.

Before picking Adrienne up, Raider looked about and listened. Neither disturbance seemed to have awakened anyone. Crazy Horse lay at his feet, out cold. Adrienne's new lover duplicated his posture behind them. She was still out.

"Damn, this seems to be my night for puttin' people t' sleep."

He leaned over and examined her by the light of the emerged moon. She was breathing deeply, evenly; she'd be out for another ten minutes at least. What he should do was locate where they were keeping the ponies, cut out his mare if he could find her, if she was still with them, and let Adrienne ride back on the gelding. Riding double all the way to Collardsville would test even the strongest mount, and since it wasn't necessary . . .

"Only it seems to be. I could poke around these woods till sunup and not find 'em. Okay, Mrs. Dubois, Adrienne, lover o' the noble savage, let's go. You and me are headin' home."

She came to before he got within a quarter mile of where he'd tied his horse. He could feel and hear her coming around and when she did he set her on her feet, holding her close when her legs threatened to give way under her.

As he expected, the instant she regained consciousness completely and recognized him she lit into him.

"You filthy beast, what do you think you're doing!"

It was clear what *she* thought he was doing; she began hammering his face with her little fists, one blow catching him in his injured windpipe. He swore, stepped clear, and swung. She crumpled with a plaintive little sigh.

"I don't wanna keep hittin' you, honest; but you're makin' me."

He carried her the rest of the way like Frances Hotaling carried her laundry across her forearms, looking down at her beautiful face, watching her sleeping peacefully when the moonlight was able to make its way through the trees to illuminate her features. When he got to his horse he tied Adrienne's wrists in front of her and tied the long end of the rope around her waist and gagged her with his bandanna. He got out of there as fast as he could, figuring that by now her lover was awake and missing her, touching bases with Crazy Horse, and forming a rescue party to chase them.

He had reached and passed the second Oglala campsite before dawn. The sky brightened but the sun did not come up; instead it resumed raining, although not nearly as hard as the day before. It was not until the camp had vanished from sight behind them that trouble, long expected and inexplicably delayed, caught up.

Almost did. they were in the middle of a long, straight stretch, the gelding's muzzle pointed south toward the distant Nebraska border, Raider looking anxiously back every hundred yards, when his concern was fulfilled. The rain was keeping the dust down and the first thing he caught sight of was a white eagle-feathered warbonnet. The second was the number of his pursuers: six. They saw him and immediately picked up speed. He cut off the road into the woods, getting deep into the trees, then cutting sharply right and moving back the way he'd come on a line parallel to the road. He rode for about twenty minutes before turning right again and making his way back to sight of the road. Dismounting, leaving Adrienne quietly fuming and assassinating him with her eyes, he moved forward on foot until he could see the road up and down for a mile or more in both directions. No sign of them. He reckoned that they'd followed him into the woods and were now searching and hopefully had not tracked his maneuvering. But he was not so sure of himself that he'd dare head back down the road past them. Better to bide his time.

Better yet, cross the road into the woods on the opposite side, and head south under that convenient cover. This he did. It was almost sunset when he decided it was safe to return to the road. By now he was beginning to pity his prisoner, which was exactly what she was, and gave in to his more humane instincts.

"If I undo your gag, will you promise to keep a cork in it?"

She nodded vigorously. She also glared.

"You gotta keep your word or *I* promise it'll go right back on. I'm not gonna go into a long song an' dance on why I'm takin' you back. We been through it all too many times, but just as much, just as hard as you don't wanna go, I gotta take you."

This explanation puzzled her for two seconds, just long enough to remind him that putting his thoughts into words wasn't exactly his strong suit.

"You know what I'm sayin'. Now do you promise, cross your heart? I mean you can talk, say whatever you like, just don't abuse my poor defenseless earpans. I mean let's be grown up. An' remember one thing: when we get back you'll be on your own. If you don't wanna stay, go back t' him, don't, it's none o' my beeswax. My job is t' bring you home an' when we get there that's the end of it. So please, try an' see my side of it. Meet me halfway, okay?"

She nodded and dispatched the fire from her eyes. He took off her gag.

"Untie me . . ."

"Oh no. I can't. How can I? You're liable t' scratch my eyes out."

"I wouldn't lower myself. I'm not an animal."

"You do want t' get away, you'll try anything. Sorry."

"Bastard!"

"That's me."

"How can you do this? Why? You've met Edgar, you know what he is."

"I keep tellin' you, that's not the point."

"I keep telling you it is!" She laughed lightly, softening her features. "I don't know why I bother discussing it, you'll never make it back to Collardsville. Standing Bear will catch up. You won't even get as far as the border."

"You're not payin' attention, lady. Your latest bunkmate already did catch up, him and his friends. They're back in the woods lookin'. I'm 'fraid they won't find us."

"Don't underestimate him, Mr. Weatherbee."

"I don't, that's why we're not lollygaggin'."

"Do you intend to keep going all night? You wouldn't do that to the poor horse, you're not *that* heartless."

"I ain't heartless period. What are you gonna do now, start feelin' sorry for yourself? That's rich, that is. You should feel sorry for yours truly, for puttin' me through this friggin' wringer when there was no need to from the start."

"My my, our feelings are hurt. I didn't ask you to come after me."

"I know. You think I'm stupid? Hey I didn't ask for the 'signment. I 'specially didn't want it after I met your lovin' husband. I'm not s'prised you don't wanna go back t' him. Only thing surprisin' is you wanna stay with the tribe. That's not surprisin', that's downright unbeliev'ble. An' crazy an' stupid t' boot!"

"Are you going to get mad again?"

"I'm not mad, lady, all I am is disgusted."

"There's nothing I can say to change your mind?"

"We're gonna stop for the night. There's a cabin 'bout a mile down outta these Hills; friends o' mine, prospector an' his wife." As the word "friend" moved from his lips to his ears he recalled Jabez the giant and imagined the pain in the back of his head visited by his fist. "The Hotalings; you'll like 'em. We'll be able t' get a hot meal, a bed for the night. Frances'll let you maybe take a bath. You'd like that, wouldn't you?"

Her face told him she was only half-listening; he could see her wheels turning faster and faster.

"Don't even think about it."

"I don't know what you're talking about. I rarely do."

"They're not gonna help you get away from me. They already know 'bout you, the only thing they don't know is you want t' stay with the tribe. Frances is a sensible soul, I won't have t' explain why I'm doin' what I got t' do. So don't bother playin' on her heartstrings or his, don't go makin' me out for your kidnapper. You'll just be wastin' your breath."

"We'll see . . ."

"You bet we will. Hey, if you'd rather, we'll just ride right on by, ride all night. We can be home lots quicker."

"You'd do that, wouldn't you, kill the poor horse just to avoid contact with people."

"Your choice, which is it gonna be?"

She shrugged. "What's the difference? We probably won't even make it to their cabin before Standing Bear catches up. If we do, your friend and his wife probably won't listen to me."

"But that won't keep you from tryin', right? On second thought, we'll stop. Yes, sir. It's about time somebody besides me tried t' talk sense into you."

She said nothing more, only smiled. He leered response. On they double-rode. Far ahead the Black Hills began to give way to reasonably level ground. In a few hours they would be crossing the Cheyenne River.

So near, he thought confidently. *And yet so far?* he added, feeling nothing like confidence.

CHAPTER TWENTY

Edgar Dubois was preparing to leave the bank for the day, brimming to overflowing with confidence in his hired guns. All day long he'd sat at his desk picturing them meeting up with Raider and Adrienne, rescuing her from the Pinkerton and answering his protests with lead. Had he only known what was actually happening with the Halliburton brothers and their friends he wouldn't have been nearly so sanguine.

At the same moment that Raider raised his eyes and saw the ground beginning to level far ahead, the four men were engaged in a conversation that was something less than either pleasant or friendly. They had pulled off the road to spend the night in the trees only to be assaulted by the first downpour; the second had caught them enroute. Edgar had come out of it with a bad cold, one of their horses—Roger's—had stepped in a hole and broken its right front fetlock joint, forcing him to put it out of its misery, forcing him to double-ride with Hannibal, since both Edgar and Ira-Vance refused to share their horses, Ira-Vance had begun whining and complaining, and despite the threats of the others, the most vicious coming from his own brother, he refused to quiet his mouth.

"I wanna go home," wailed Ira-Vance. "I'm catchin' your cold, Ed, I'm gettin' the shaketh, I should be abed, we never will find her, we could look for a year and not."

"Shut up!" snapped his brother. "I'm sick and tired o' your gripin'!"

"We won't. She'th prob'ly not even up there, she could be anyplathe . . ."

"He's right about that," interposed Wizlowski bluntly.

"Don't you start, Roger," snarled Edgar.

"I will if I like."

"I'm the leader!"

"Some leader. You got us lost for better that half a day. That Pinkerton could have rescued her and gone right by us while we were wandering around in the woods . . ."

"He'th right!" chirped Ira-Vance.

"I said shut up! All o' ya. Act like a grown-up man, Ira-Vance, think about the money, five hundred dollars, more money than you're like to see your whole life. Cash. From the banker. He's got it, he's rich as hell, Chrissakes, and he wants her back so much he'll pay five times that, maybe ten times . . ." He stopped short. All three were studying him. "I got me an idea."

"I know what you're thinking," said Wizlowski. "We rescue her and *we* hold her for ransom."

"What are you talkin' about?" burst Edgar. "What ransom? You're disgustin', you know that? Wherever did you get such a disgustin' idea? All I'm sayin' is Dubois wants her back so bad he can taste it, if we ask him polite-like for a thousan' dollars, he'll pay it. You just see if he won't, Roger Wizlowski."

Hannibal was reining up. "Somebody coming," he bawled. "I can hear plain."

"Get off the road!" snapped Edgar. "Over there to those trees. Move!"

Away they thundered, vanishing into the woods. Edgar was the first to pull up, jump down, and run to a tree he could hide behind and gain a clear view of the road. The others followed his lead.

"It's her!" Wizlowski rasped excitedly.

"How the hell you know that?" grumbled Edgar.

"She looks just like what Dubois described her," ventured Hannibal.

"That'th the Pinkerton with her," said Ira-Vance.

Abruptly finding himself outvoted, Edgar capitulated. He checked his iron, then reholstered it.

"Let's go get 'em . . ."

"Wait, wait," said Wizlowski. "Let's figure this out, let's do it right."

Edgar gaped blankly. "How?"

"He's moving real slow, why don't I catch up with them, stop them, talk to her, you know, hold them up, give you boys time to get well ahead, and when we go on you can bushwack us."

"That'th a great idea!" burst Ira-Vance.

His brother's expression testified that he didn't share his enthusiasm, but he grudgingly gave in.

"Go run 'em, down, Roger. Hannibal, you'll ride double with Ira-Vance."

"Doth he have to?" whined Ira-Vance as Hannibal obediently dismounted.

Wizlowski didn't wait to hear how they'd ride. He was gone. Reaching the road, he caught up as quickly as he could.

"Mrs. Dubois?" he asked, politely removing his hat.

"Who are you?" Raider asked. "What d' you want?"

"I'm Mrs. Dubois," said Adrienne.

"Thank God, we'd just about given up hope. Your husband's beside himself worrying about you . . ."

"We?" asked Raider, slit-eyeing him suspiciously. "Anwer the question. Who are you an' what d' you want?"

"Isn't it obvious?" she snapped. "Numbskull. You, whatever your name is, untie me. And get out that gun before he shoots you! Do it!"

Wizlowski gulped with surprise, but complied. A bit tardily, Raider had already gotten his out.

"She's a little bit crazy with the heat, friend," he explained. "Believe it or not, she fell in love with the Injuns back there, with ever'body who'd climb in bed with 'er. She wanted t' stay. I had t' tie her t' . . ."

"He's lying! Don't listen to him! He captured me, had his way with me, abused and tortured me! Now he's taking me back. Not to Collardsville. To nearby. He intends to hold me for ransom! Save me! Save me! I beg you!"

"She's fulla . . ."

It was as far as Raider got. Three riders, two sharing

one mount, came galloping toward them, irons out and waving. Two fired, then the third. Raider ducked instinctively.

"Drop it!" bellowed Wizlowski.

And before Raider could, Wizlowski fired, knocking the Colt from his grasp.

"You sonovabitch..."

The three newcomers arrived. Without a word Hannibal began untying her.

"Mrs. Dubois," said Edgar. "Edgar Halliburton's the name. Your husban' hired us to find you and crown me for the king o' France if we haven't!"

"Kill him! Kill him!" she screamed, pointing at Raider. "He raped me!"

"You dirty bastard," growled Edgar and swung, narrowly missing Raider, who ducked just in time. "Take care o' the lady, boys, I got bus'ness with this one." He leveled his six-gun at Raider's belt buckle. "Get 'em up high as they go, Mister. Now turn round and march. Over to the trees there."

"You're makin' the biggest mistake o' your life, Shitkicker!"

Edgar pushed him, hurrying his step. Neither looked back before they reached the trees. Moving into them, Edgar pushed him a second time. Raider nearly fell, catching hold of a tree trunk just in time.

"Move!" snapped his captor.

Raider weighed his chances. They came up badly out of balance. The gun at his back was at least six or eight feet behind him. The man wielding it didn't strike him as overly brilliant, but he was smart enough to keep a safe distance between them. On and on they trudged.

"Okay, this is far 'nough," said Edgar. "Turn around; you wouldn't want me shootin' you in the back, wouldja?"

Raider turned, his hands still upraised. His left arm was tiring rapidly from the wound in his bicep.

"You shoot me and you'll hang sure as you're standin' there," he said, trying his best to sound threatening and unruffled at the same time. Edgar snickered.

"Who's gonna tell? Her? You attacked her, you bastard, you think she's gonna' put a damn rope 'round my neck? Me who saved her from you? Your brains must be scrambled."

"Let me put down my hands, okay?"

"Go ahead, condemned man's last request, right?"

Raider lowered his hands. Edgar took one step backwards, widening the distance between them to nearly ten feet. He lifted his gun, bringing the muzzle up to Raider's breastbone. He cocked.

"How do you want it? In the chest or the head? Whatever you say..."

"Just get it over with, you sonovabitch."

Raider's mouth dried up in seconds. It was crammed with cotton. Sweat coursed down his body under his shirt. His pounding heart threatened to rip his breast pocket. He tried to swallow and couldn't, Standing Bear's near destruction of his windpipe preventing it.

Edgar leered and raised his gun to Raider's face.

And fired. The sound hammered Raider's eardrums. But it did not come from the gun pointed at him. Amazed, shocked rigid, he watched his would-be executioner's smirk fade from his face, supplanted by astonishment, saw his eyes climb upwards in their sockets, the gun tilt downward, his knees give way.

"You okay, Sittin' Bull?" croaked a familiar voice.

Before he turned to confirm where it was coming from he sucked his lungs full of the sweet air in a momentous, a gargantuan sigh of relief. And instantly regretted it. The speaker came up to him, bringing his familiar, outrageously foul stench.

"Amory..." burst Raider. "Amory Wiggins!"

"In the flesh. Well, you gonna thank me for savin' your life or what?"

"God in heaven and all his angels, was that close! How? Where?"

"Been followin' you. 'Bout four mile. Eleanor an' Harold's over there." He indicated a spot about halfway back to the road. "We was up the way about a hunnert yards when they came up t' you. The first one set you up, you know. I wanted t' catch up t' tell you I found gold. Up by Jewel Cave." He paused and winked mischievously. "Ain't sayin' where 'zactly. It's not Sutter's Mill, but it's not too shabby. I'm headin' back down t' Collardsville t' file my claim and hire me some help."

Raider saw no reason to remind him that he was trespassing on Sioux land, that nobody in Collardsville or anywhere else would permit him to file a claim, that any stakes he put up weren't worth the sweat it took to drive them into place; the man had just saved his life, why douse his dreams with cold water? Then again, maybe he knew something Raider did not.

Amory was reloading the single chamber he had emptied into Raider's captor.

"Grab his gun there," he said, "let's go back and take care o' his three friends." He grinned toothlessly. "We can s'prise 'em easy. They heerd the one shot. They got to think it was him killin' you."

"We got an edge, that's true," said Raider, "but let's not rush things."

He retrieved and checked Edgar's gun, slipping it into his holster.

"What you wanna do?" queried Amory.

Before Raider could respond, gunfire erupted back on the road. The trees were so thick neither could see what was going on. Raider ran toward the sound, his rescuer right behind him. They pulled up short behind trees. The shooting kept up, but it was not coming from the road. Puffs of smoke showed at the edge of the woods. Neither could see a soul until a flash of white passed from one tree to another across from where they'd seen the smoke.

"Standin' Bear!" blurted Raider. And answered Amory's puzzled look. "One o' the Oglalas, her latest Romeo. I interrupted their screwin', whacked 'im over the head an' pulled 'im off her. Him and his friends already caught up with us once. I outfoxed 'em."

"Not good 'nough it looks like."

"Jesus Christ," moaned Raider. "If this don't beat all. I

come through the hottest hell and highest high water, get 'er this far, now sure as you're born she'll get hit by a stray bullet, I'll wind up fetchin' in her corpse, if I fetch 'er in at all! Damn!"

"Thunderation! You give up quick as you fly off the pump handle. Relax. Those boys ain't 'bout t' give 'er up 'thout a fight an' her boy friend's the last person in the world wants 'er hurt. She's in no danger. You wanna worry 'bout somebody, worry 'bout the dead fellow's sidekicks. How many Injuns follyed you down?"

"At least six, maybe more come after 'em."

"Six'll do 'gainst them cracker barrel cowboys. Unless..."

"What?" Raider eyed him worriedly.

"She takes it into her head t' screw things up. You did say one o' them Injuns was her boyfriend."

"Maybe one o' the town boys'll get smart an' knock 'er cold," said Raider hopefully. "Cover her with pine needles so's Standin' Bear can't see..."

"Whatta you say we get on over there?"

"They're sure t' see us crossin' the road," Raider rejoined.

They ran forward about a quarter mile before crossing, Raider crossing his fingers as he sprinted into the trees opposite, praying that the Indians, who were facing in that direction, would be too busy to notice or care if they did. Gaining the cover of the woods, both swung right, heading for the fight, intending to join the three and Adrienne and help drive away the braves.

"I just hope she hasn't screwed things up already," muttered Raider as he ran. "She sure knows how..."

Closer and closer came the sound of firing. It sounded to Raider as if the Indians were giving as good as they were getting when somebody barely fifty feet ahead screamed and died.

"That was a white man," said Amory.

He was right, Raider mused. Seconds later his most dreaded worry was confirmed. The situation blew up in his face. They came upon the three white men, all dead. Ira-

Vance had been shot in the face with an arrow, the point snapping his cheekbone, pulling the shaft a good five inches upward into his brain. He'd also been shot in the chest. The entire left side of Hannibal's face had been blown away, eye and all. It looked like somebody had laid him down and chopped it away with an axe. Roger Wizlowski, the decoy, had been gut shot. Examining him, they discovered he was still breathing, but dying and in agony. Not a six-gun was in sight.

"Injuns got all their hardware," rasped Amory. "Wouldn'cha know..."

Adrienne was nowhere to be seen.

"Where is she?" Raider snapped at Wizlowski.

"With them," he gasped.

"They got 'er..." murmured Amory resignedly.

Wizlowski tried to shake his head, tried to speak further, but could do neither. His suffering ceased, he died, the last red thread of his life spilling out the corner of his mouth.

"They didn't get her," said Raider to Amory. "That's what he was tryin' to say. She slipped away from this bunch, circled round and ran straight into Standin' Bear's arms. Bet the ranch on it. Come on, let's get my horse an' one o' theirs for you an' go after 'em."

They ran toward the edge of the woods to within sight of the road just in time to see the Indians beating them to the standing horses. Astride their ponies, they were collecting all four. Raider steadied his gun and fired; Amory's shot echoed his. Two braves dropped, screaming, from their mounts. Confusion seized the others, including Standing Bear and Adrienne, who had gotten off his pony and was trying to climb onto the gelding. It whirled nervously in a circle and white-eyed her as she tried and tried. The four Indians had two rifles in addition to bows and arrows and the pistols taken from Wizlowski and the others. As Raider looked on, Adrienne spotted his pistol still lying where it had fallen. She snatched it up and began firing at him. H ducked just in time as two shots whistled overhead, thudding into the tree behind him. Amory was already flat on Raider's left, using a tree for cover. Raider threw himself down, scudding like a crab for a rock about five feet from him.

The Indians and Adrienne, meanwhile, had downed five of the ponies and horses and were using them for cover. Caught up in the excitement, Adrienne quickly emptied Raider's own gun at him. She came closest with her first two shots and the fifth and sixth were completely wild, so impatient was she to kill. He watched her pull the trigger on an empty chamber, flare in anger, and toss away the gun. Then he gasped aloud. She stood up and began waving both arms, calling to him. The brave closest to her reached up, clutched a handful of her skirt and pulled her tumbling down.

"Gotcha!" boomed Amory.

Sure enough, he hit a third brave full in the throat, his pilfered six-gun glinting as it fell from his hand.

"Good boy," called Raider.

The two with the rifles returned fire, the shots so close they sounded like one.

"Keep down!" cautioned Raider.

The brave alongside Standing Bear wielding two six-guns whooped loudly, rising just high enough as he did so for Raider to pot him. His two seconds of triumph died with him.

"Amory..." Raider called.

No response. Raider sucked air between clenched teeth, held it, and looked over at the old man. The base of the tree trunk hid his head; Raider did not need to see his face, the way his body lay confirmed he was dead. It was so relaxed it looked like it had been poured on the ground. Raider groaned.

"Dammit to hell..."

A bullet hit his rock, chipping it, the chip skinning his temple. He ducked too late, cursed, shook off the stinging, brought his fingers down with blood on the tips, sneaked a quick look around the other side and spied barely a half inch of the tops of two heads; Standing Bear's and the one other survivor's. Even as he saw them, both lowered from sight. Adrienne, her gun empty and no other within safe reach, was already down. Was she okay? he wondered. Could she have been hit? No. He hadn't fired anywhere near her; he'd been very careful not to. Amory hadn't fired period, not since he'd killed the fourth brave, his third, and that was a split-second after one of them pulled her down.

So now it was down to two to one, the same odds as the baggage car shootout two weeks before, just outside Cartwood. Two years ago it seemed like, so much had happened since. Again Raider glanced in Amory's direction, and a wave of sadness welled and rolled in his chest.

"If you hadn'ta showed up an' saved my skin, you wouldn'ta lost your own, stinkin' old coot..."

He broke his iron and refilled the empty cylinders. Just in time. The two Indians were rising slowly. Raider leveled and aimed, but held his fire when he saw what Standing Bear was up to. He had pulled her up in front of him and was using her as a shield, leering broadly over her shoulder, the muzzle of his gun set against her temple. She looked panic-stricken.

"So much for love at first sight," muttered Raider.

The other survivor was also on his feet, standing grinning about two feet from Standing Bear and his shield. Raider took quick stock. He had started lowering his iron when Standing Bear pulled Adrienne up in front of him, but the sight of the other Oglala standing in the clear was too tempting to ignore.

He shot and killed him.

"S'prise, s'prise."

As the sound cracked across the open space to the road Standing Bear's leer soured into a scowl. He suddenly seemed torn, but Raider knew he wouldn't shoot her. He might have wanted to, but it made no sense; why sacrifice his own protection? Raider was confident he would not when he shot the other. Who had been just as confident that Raider would hold his fire when he stood up.

"Why wouldja think that, stupid?"

Raider waved his gun, aching, itching to shoot, but afraid to, Standing Bear's head was so close to hers. He began backing away, pulling her along. She did not protect, did not utter a sound, or even turn to look at him; she kept her eyes fixed on the rock behind which Raider lay.

"Bastard... he'll get away for sure."

He looked like he would. Leaving the horses and ponies, unable to manage them, holding her as he was, making for the cover of the woods, planning—Raider was sure—to get well into them, and then, while Raider was pursuing, he'd double back and retrieve two horses.

"You're makin' a big mistake, Romeo. Tell him, Jooliet."

Raider waited, then got slowly up, tensing, expecting a bullet, prepared to drop if he had to. None came. Holstering his gun, he ran across to the ponies and horses, now all back up on their feet, caught the reins of the gelding and a horse for her, and ran them into the woods down a ways to his right, tying them to the same tree in deep enough so that they could not be seen from the road.

Then he started back through the woods, gun cocked and ready, moving stealthily from tree to tree, now and then stopping, standing stock still and listening. Not a sound, not so much as a single twig cracking underfoot. Sweat started and a finger of fear traced its way lightly up his spine. The trees were dense, but every other step he showed himself and instinct warned him that his quarry was no longer fleeing, but had positioned himself in a well-concealed spot and was patiently waiting for him to show himself.

It was a dicey situation, and getting dicier by the minute. If he hadn't the sense to realize that, he thought worriedly, his sweat glands and his heart were conspiring to tell him.

But he got unexpected help. His pounding heart leaped gleefully at the shrill sound of her voice. They had become separated, either that or Standing Bear had ditched her. She was calling pleadingly for him, calling him darling, dearest.

"Man, that woman sure has a way with Injuns."

On second thought it was the other way around.

"Darling... darling..."

She was drawing closer. Raider got an idea. Holstering his iron, he climbed a tree, pulling himself up, branch by branch, until he was about fifteen feet up. Positioning himself, he could look down. He could hear her coming, her footsteps between her calls. Standing Bear heard her and was approaching, coming back from deeper in the woods. Looking down, Raider watched him come up to her. He was livid, growling at her angrily.

"Darling..."

He rushed up to her, grabbed her and began choking her. Raider could feel his own windpipe suddenly begin aching, recalling *his* encounter with those hands.

"Let her go, you sonovabitch!"

Standing Bear froze, his hands still clamping her throat. She had dropped to her knees. She had hold of his wrists and was trying to break his grip. Both looked upward. Raider had his gun out.

"Let her go!" he bawled.

Standing Bear did, stepping back, pulling his gun from his waist, bringing it up swiftly. But not swiftly enough. Raider fired. The slug hit just inside his right shoulder, driving deep into his chest. A hideous scowl seized his features as he tried to shake it off. She screamed, her hands flying to her mouth; she fainted. Raider aimed to fire a follow-up shot, but there was no need. Standing Bear fell dead.

CHAPTER TWENTY ONE

She was still unconscious when Raider set her down near where he'd tied the two horses. As a precaution he had tied her wrists and ankles, then left her and recrossed the road to where Amory lay dead. He dug a shallow grave in the soft ground and buried him as best he could. The others, including his would-be executioner, he left where they'd died. He scattered the Indians' ponies and the three horses, saving the fourth for her.

By the time he got back to her she was awake and struggling with her bindings.

"Untie me, you filthy bastard!"

"You want your gag back?"

"No!" she screamed.

"Then shut up. You got 'leven people killed, countin' the latest light o' your life. Countin', too, one o' the nicest old gaffers that ever drew breath, who it so happens saved my life. I've had enough o' your goddamn wildness and your mouth, your stupid opinions o' me. I'm takin' you home if I gotta tie an' gag you every step o' the way." He leaned close and glared fiercely. "If I gotta knock you cold an' keep you that way, you savvy? You savvy!"

"There's no need to shout."

"The hell there ain't. You behave yourself or you just may not make it back to Edgar's lovin' arms. Along 'bout now I don't muchly care if you do, and if you die out here tryin' t' get away or whatever, nobody'll ever know what happened, so keep that in mind if you get any clever ideas, savvy!"

"I can hear you."

"I'm gonna untie your ankles so you can ride. We're leavin' now an' no stops till we get there. I changed my mind about layin' over at the Hotalings."

"I'll never make it, I'm exhausted."

"Bullshit, you got the stamina of a friggin' mountain lion."

She was staring at him, her expression visibly softening, the fire deserting her eyes, replaced by a sensuous, yearning look.

"I'm sorry, Mr. Weatherbee, for everything. I truly am. You're quite right. I'm solely responsible for all the carnage, all your problems, everything I've done to impede you. I can't blame you for hating me."

With this she began to whimper. She went on through it.

"I'm sorry, I'm so sorry..."

"Oh for Chris... cryin' out loud, don't start that."

"It's just that to have to go back to him like this. In disgrace, my life, my reputation in shreds."

"Hey, nobody's gonna know from me what you did with He-Dog, with him... I got my faults, but I'm no blabbermouth. And there's sure nobody else left alive t' tattle on you."

He had knelt beside her; he patted her back consolingly. Suddenly, as quickly as she had changed moods, she changed back, recoiling from his touch, glaring viciously at him.

"You keep your filthy hands to yourself, you bastard. You scum! You raped me, you pig, and I intend to trumpet it to the whole world!"

He said not a word. He just stood up, sighed, got out his bandanna, flung it once to separate it, rolled it up and gagged her.

"'Leven dead and she survives. If there's any justice in this friggin' world it sure don't come round these parts. Come on, Mrs. Dubois, you and me are headin' home. And thanks..."

Through her continuing fury her face said she didn't understand. He explained.

"When that clown marched me off into the woods t' hang my brains on a tree with a slug, thanks for speakin' up for me. One word from you woulda stopped 'im in 'is tracks, he wouldn'ta dared t' kill me. Only you were all for it, weren'tcha? Thanks, Joo-liet, thanks a lot."

CHAPTER TWENTY TWO

Sheriff Meshach Gatling's final effort to dislodge himself from his chair was successful. He waddled to the window and looked out. His eyes had not deceived him; Edgar Dubois, leather protector, imperious manner, snobbish mien, and all, was coming out of the bank and heading his way.

"Oh dear," muttered Gatling to himself. "This is all I need, a couple hours of his whinin' to make my day."

He opened the door and stood aside and gaped in amazement. Edgar came striding in, his face flooded with the most amiable of grins, and greeting him effusively.

"Meshach, Meshach, Meshach, isn't it a lovely day? Exquisite! An absolute gem..."

He took the sheriff's chair uninvited, dropping into it, pulling his trousers up to avoid bagging the knees, crossing his legs, relaxing and eyeing Gatling. On his face was the most contented look the sheriff had ever seen there. The first contented look he'd ever seen, now that he thought about it.

"Good news?" he asked.

"The next best thing," said Edgar expansively. "I did a lot of thinking about this unhappy affair last night and I've decided everything's going to turn out all right. The Halliburton brothers and their friends will find Adrienne and bring her back, restore her to the bosom of her family."

What family is that? wondered Gatling, but said not a word. On rolled his visitor.

"If you think about it, I mean really put your mind to it, the only possible ending is a happy one."

Gatling wanted very much to disagree, but again held his tongue.

"The savages won't hurt her; according to my research on the subject of white women abducted by Indians, a whopping eight-five percent either escape, are rescued, or traded for and returned to their loved ones. Eighty-five percent!"

Gatling had no idea where Dubois got his figures and his first instinct was to question them, but he said nothing. He was a kindly man, ever wary of hurting people's feelings or their egos, and at the moment, felt no great urge to shadow Edgar's smile with his opinion on the subject.

Edgar waggled a finger, gently pounding home his point.

"Most important is my men's motivation. Their sort would kill for ready cash. They'll go through the fires of hell to rescue her and bring her back. Why for five hundred they'd probably kill each other!"

Gatling didn't think they'd go that far; but on second thought he agreed it was possible, knowing the four as he did.

"What happens in most cases is that the savages become bored with their captives. And all the while, of course, there's the threat of retribution on a scale far larger than their crime warrants. Do you know that in the case of Annie Hepburn, an emigrant's wife and mother of four, kidnapped by the Apaches just last year, the Department of Arizona sent out two full troops of cavalry to rescue her? What they ended up doing was bartering horses for her release, but when she crossed over to the protection of the soldiers the officer in charge immediately gave the order to charge. They attached the Indians and in two hours massacred every man, woman, and child."

"You told me you didn't want to alert the army."

"I didn't, and I don't regret that one whit. If you'll just let me finish making my point here. Word of that massacre must have spread all over the territories. The Oglalas heard, I'm certain; the way I see it when the party that captured Adrienne brought her back to the main camp, whoever the chief of chiefs is, the overall man in charge, probably recoiled in horror at the sight of her."

Gatling quelled the urge to laugh in his face. There was, he reminded himself, no limit to the stupidity of the uninitiated.

"His first thought was to return her. And my guess is he would have, only something happened to delay things. The tribe ran into trouble of some kind. Most important of all, Meshach, what absolutely inspires me with confidence is right here..."

He thumped his chest.

"My feelings, my conviction that all will turn out well. So many factors contribute. My hired hands' motivations, the savages' awareness based on the experience of other Indians that the game isn't worth the candle, Adrienne's resourcefulness—she's really quite intelligent for a woman—and the certainty that people, not even savages, don't kill or harm without good reason, unless they have something to gain."

"Oh for Chrissakes..."

Edgar jerked his head up and stared hard at Gatling, a glower of resentment forming on his face.

"You disagree?"

Gatling suddenly wished very much to bite his tongue for letting it slip so carelessly. Advising the man that he was talking through his hat—that he didn't know what in the world he was talking about—seemed both fruitless and unnecessary. Yet this was a man not only accustomed to getting his own way in everything, not only incapable of accepting disagreement with his opinions, but so woefully ignorant of what he was up against, to even suggest that he might be deluding himself would undoubtedly fire his anger and resentment, and trigger a tirade of sarcasm and insult in reprisal. It would be utter folly to confront him with the truth.

What, for that matter, was the truth? What was going on out there? Had Raider managed to get to her before the four misfits? Before she was killed or so badly maimed she'd kill herself? Gatling wished he knew, merely to satisfy his own curiousity, not inform her idiot husband.

"I don't disagree, Mr. Dubois," he replied quietly. "How can I? Who knows what's happening? I couldn't begin to guess..."

Again Edgar thumped his chest. And beamed confidently. *"I know.* My little voice tells me."

Your little voice is fulla... Gatling jettisoned the comment from his thoughts, before it got out of control and into words.

"I can't help saying I do worry 'bout her, o' course," he went on. "But I worry 'bout Raider, too."

Edgar's expression in response to this was that of a man who'd bitten into rotten fruit.

"You're not serious. That misfit tramp? Oh, we had our differences, I fired him, replaced him with the Halliburtons and the others. We never did see eye to eye on this thing, but I wouldn't wish him dead or badly hurt."

Mighty white of you, reflected Gatling.

"I just don't want him getting in the way of the others. If I find out he did, so help me I'll hand his head back to Pinkerton on a plate!"

Sure you will, mused Gatling, *day before yesterday. Chrissakes, you're not man enough to shoot him in the back, much less face up to him.*

His face betrayed his inner feelings. Edgar eyed him.

"Is something wrong?"

"No, no. If you'll excuse me, Mr. Dubois, I got to go out. I skipped breakfast and my stomach's starting to bawl me out..."

He reached for his hat. Edgar got up from the chair.

"I'll come with you. We can have a bite at the hotel. They always save me the corner table by that hideous potted palm. They're featuring fresh oysters this week all the way from the Atlantic Coast. Lead the way, I'm right behind you. I've only scratched the surface, there's so much, so many angles to this thing, I could talk your ear off!"

It was night when they rode past the Hotalings. The house was in darkness. Adrienne noticed him looking at it, and easily guessed who lived there. Earlier Raider had relented and removed her gag. She was behaving herself for the time being, not burning his ears with insults, not spouting off in general, but he'd come to know her quite well, and knew that whatever mood she put on, whatever behavior—good, bad, spiteful, venomous—it could change in a second. Doc Weatherbee would know what doctors called that quirk in a person; he knew all sorts of things like that.

But she was behaving herself at the moment.

"That's your friends' place, isn't it?"

"Yeah. They're asleep. Wouldn't be very friendly to wake 'em up, would it?"

"I'm so tired I'm having trouble staying on this horse's back. I can't keep my eyes open."

"We can stop at sunup and rest a couplea hours."

"That's five hours from now..."

"Only a couple."

"You said they're your friends, don't you want to see them? I'm sure they want to see you."

"Look, if you're thinkin' 'bout tryin' t' make a break for it, do me a favor and do it with me solo; don't try to ring in innocent parties, Chrissakes."

"You do have the foulest mouth."

"I know, you tol' me. And it's people like you make people like me foul-mouthed. You rub me the wrongest way I have ever been rubbed!"

"What did I do? Oh, I've been a handful, I know..."

"Handful? Hey, a little kid that cries all the time an' won't eat his spinach, that's a handful; you, lady, are the biggest pain in the neck an' six other places on God's green earth."

"But you like me. Certainly enough to take advantage of me."

"Me? It was the other way round; besides, we already covered that 'bout sixteen times. Talk 'bout somethin' else if you have t' talk. Tell me what you're gonna do when we get back. You gonna have it out with him, leave him? Go back to Hartford?"

"I really can't see that that's any concern of yours, Weatherbee."

"My name is Raider."

"You told Chief Crazy Horse..."

"I know. It's Raider. Weatherbee was an old pardner o' mine."

She did not speak for the next five minutes. The darkened cabin faded into the gloom behind them. He retreated into his thoughts, shutting her out. He thought about Crazy Horse and his people and pictured them trekking west toward the Powder River country, abandoning the Oglalas' land by treaty to the white scavengers. When and with who would he make his stand? The other Sioux would join forces with him and the Cheyenne; maybe even the Pawnees, although their chief, Sky Chief, was no friend of Crazy Horse's, Red Cloud's, or Sitting Bull's. Still, sometimes circumstances do make strange alliances necessary.

She broke into his thoughts.

"When will we get to Collardsville? Tell me how many miles, I can figure it out."

"From sunrise, allowin' for one good long rest, we should be there late tomorrow."

"Late tomorrow? And you wanted to ride straight through without stopping?"

"What I want is t' get this nonsense over with soon as we can. Hey, I'm willin' t' stop up the line so you can get a couplea hours sleep, maybe eat some biscuits, heat up some coffee; you know how far it is, you came this way up, didn'cha? Or did you sleep from the berry patch to the caves?"

"Must you be so sarcastic? Downright insolent at times."

"Oh geez, I'm sorry, I forgot I'm travelin' with the friggin' Queen o' England. Pardon me, Your Majesty.

"You're not doing yourself any good, you know. When I tell Edgar some of the things you've done."

"Tell him. Tell him how I raped you. I don't care. The people I care 'bout would never believe you. You can lie yourself blue, it's water off a duck t' me. You're not the first spoiled-rotten, snooty, know-it-all, bigmouth lady la-de-da I tangled with. Hell, one time I got messed up in spades with the Queen of Montenegro. For actin' high an' mighty, she makes you look like the friggin' little match girl, rags, no shoes, an' all. I've known dozens o' women wouldn' want you t' wash their feet!"

"Indeed..."

"Indeed! I'll admit one thing, though, I never met one before who can turn on the sweetness an' light and then switch it off, an' turn on the nastiness an' rotten viciousness so quick as you. I think you got some pretty important parts loose upstairs, lady."

"I'm not interested in what you think."

"That's it, stick your nose in the air. You look friggin' ridic'lous, you know that? All tuckered up like a raggedy rubbish picker, dirty face, hair all a mess, haven't seen soap an' water in two weeks, and you're still the queen, right?"

"Breeding can be artfully disguised, but once it's in you it survives in perpetuity."

"Perpetu'ty, la-de-da."

She scowled hatefully. "Filthy tramp, grub, ignoramus! Although, I admit, not a complete one. You at least have sense enough not to untie my wrists. I don't advise you to; you do and I'll steal your gun and blow your head off!"

"Oh balony, you ain't man 'nough. Wouldn't have the guts. That's where you and ol' Edgar are as alike as two peas, both big talkers, big mouths outside, soft as rotten grapes in. Pick up the pace there, you can talk an' ride at a decent clip at the same time. Your horse ain't even listenin'."

The sun rose over Lame Johnny Creek and seemed to hesitate before starting its climb into the pale blue sky; unusually pale, as if the darkness had drained all but a faint tinge of it, taking it along when it departed. Raider let her ride ahead so he could keep an eye on her. She had not uttered a sound for about two hours. She had to be exhausted and earlier had griped about being so, but as grubby as she looked there was no sign of fatigue in her face.

"Pull up, we're stoppin'."

He built a fire by the side of the road and while it flamed and burned down to embers, hobbled both horses in the grass and gave them water. She lay on the ground pretending to sleep. He knew she was faking it. He got out the biscuits, what was left of his coffee, and the little japanned pot and his cup and readied them. Then he stood over her.

"I'm gonna untie your wrists so you can eat proper."

"Aren't you afraid I'll steal your gun?"

"Not really." He grinned. "Maybe I'm what you called me back there, a ig, ignor..."

"Ignoramus. Ignorant person, a dunce."

"You learn those big words back in finishin' school? An' like 'bastard'? You got a pretty filthy mouth for all your highfalutin' airs. Here..."

He undid her wrists. She massaged them. They weren't red, weren't raw, didn't need massaging the way he'd tied them: securely without being too tight. She rubbed and rubbed and put on a pained expression. It was all he could do to keep from snickering. When she was done she sat picking at the grass aimlessly and averting her eyes.

"Hey, I didn't let you loose for that. Make yourself useful, fix the coffee. I'll sharpen a little stick so's we can toast the biscuits."

They ate in silence. She was proud, but not too proud to share his meager fare. Every so often he caught her rubbing her backside and grimacing slightly. Once she saw him watching and stopped so quickly he laughed.

"If it's hurtin' you now, wait till we come in sight o' Collardsville. Course if it gets too bad, you can always walk."

"I might. I'm an excellent rider, superb; it's just that it's such a long way."

"It's nothin'. Try ridin' from San Antonio to Monterey, Mexico sometime. A thousan' miles straight as string, dry, barren. At least this road you got somethin' t' look at. Look over there, see that little fella lookin' straight at you, wonderin' what a grand lady like you is doin' out here in the wilds? That's a chestnut-back chickadee. Isn't his little brown cap cute? Hey, bird . . ."

The chickadee jerked its head up and down twice and flew off.

"He's not interested," said Adrienne. "I can't say I blame him."

"He was lookin' at you."

They ate. He let her sleep for two hours, woke her up and they got back on the road. They crossed the border around sundown. By now the two of them were worn out and even their horses showed signs of tiring, despite their not pushing them. Raider changed his mind.

"We'll sleep tonight."

"Where?"

"The Palace Hotel," he snorted. "Where you think? Under a tree in case it rains. It looks like it could. That's all we need. I'm really beat; I could use three or four hours, so I'm sorry but I'm 'fraid I'm gonna have t' tie you back up."

"Please don't! I give you my word I won't try anything."

"I wish I believed you, but I don't."

"Where would I go? I wouldn't know how to get back to their camp. Besides, you know as well as I, after what happened Crazy Horse would never accept me back."

"They're not there anyhow; they were gettin' ready to pull out when we left. Headin' for the Powder River country. Lady, I'm not worried 'bout you runnin' back t' them, what I worry about is closin' my eyes on you with yours still open and my gun within reach. I really would resent your blowin' my head off."

"I wouldn't do such a barbarous thing!"

"Desp'rate people never do know how far they can go and civ'lized people walk round with a lotta animal in 'em, clawin' like fury to get out."

"Ahhh, the saddle tramp philosopher, the diamond in the rough. Please, tie me if you insist, but do spare me your illiterate rambling."

"Sure."

"Mr. Weatherbee, Raider, whatever your real name is, permit me to say you are an unchivalrous bastard!"

"I know, you already tol' me. Many times."

"You punch me, hurt me physically, stubbornly refuse to even consider my position, my rights as a human being, ignore my pleas, you reduce me to wretchedness and gloat over it. You are the most hateful, detestable man I have ever had the misfortune to meet. You disgust me."

"Right. Let's go, pick up the pace. At the rate we're goin', we won't get you back till Christmas."

CHAPTER TWENTY THREE

They slept that night by Hat Creek. They were both able to bathe, using fine sand in place of soap. He trusted her out of his sight behind a thicket on the bank. At sunup they were back on the road. He had been in her company now long enough to assess her, evaluate her in terms of good points and bad, but the one thing he could not do was anticipate her changes in mood. She never gave him a clue, and she blew as hot and cold as a March wind.

Knowing her as he'd come to he wasn't surprised when she greeted him warly upon awakening, helped prepare breakfast, and spared him any sarcasm and insults. In their place he expected her to make one last play for him, come on to him, weaken his defenses, get him hot and bothered and off-balance. Get his manhood up and his guard down, and then kill him with whatever was handy, not excluding his own gun.

But she did not take this tack. Instead, for the first time since they started out from the scene of the showdown, she seemed to resign herself to her defeat. They rode side by side, her hands free, her brightness and beauty returned, her energy restored by sleep.

"May I say something?"

This startled him; she'd never before asked permission to speak.

"What?"

"You'll admit you've been hard on me. I'll admit, I suppose, the circumstances have warranted it." She smiled. "I've asked for it. In your heart I know you think you're doing the right thing, bringing me back. From your point of view you are. You're a brave man, maybe that's what makes me so angry."

His face when he looked her way said he didn't understand.

"Rather frustrated. I can't help comparing you and Edgar. You certainly are light years apart. I picture him doing some of the things you've done these past few days and it's just so ludicrous it almost makes me laugh out loud. Yes, you think you're doing the right thing; everybody else thinks so too, I'm sure. Only sometimes the right thing can be so horribly wrong. Heartlessly wrong."

"You mean like when a little kid's colt that he loves with all his heart busts a leg and has to be shot..."

"More like when a marriage is arranged as they are in India and lots of other countries. Where the boy and girl don't even know each other and they're forced to marry for every reason the parents can think of. Every reason except the most important."

"I get that. Was that the way it was with you an' him?"

"Oh no, I went into it with my eyes wide open. I knew what he was. I flattered myself I could change him."

"People can't never change people."

"Oh, I couldn't agree more. Now. Remember my telling you that day when I was out berrying I'd made up my mind to leave him? Divorce him? It's true."

"So what's the problem? Go back an' divorce 'im, go back t' Hartford."

"You don't understand, he'd never agree to a divorce, his ego wouldn't allow it. Out here it's not like back East. People who hate each other with a passion stick together. They have to."

"Why?"

"Isn't it obvious? For appearances. Edgar is a pillar of the community, the town banker. How would it look to people if he and his wife split up?"

"Who cares how it looks?"

"*He* does. Don't get me wrong. I'm certainly going to try, but he'll fight it every step of the way. And in the end, oh God..."

Sympathy surged in him, filling his heart. He suddenly felt so sorry for her he wanted to lean over and pull her close to him, pat her shoulder consolingly, talk to her with compassion, tell her how sorry he was. But he did not.

"It may not turn out as bad as you figger," he said encouragingly.

"It'll be worse."

"One thing; goin' t' live with the Injuns, takin' up their ways, their life, a white person tryin' t' make it their own, don't never work."

"You're wrong, terribly wrong. When they captured me, my first reaction was fright, of course. I was scared speechless, but at the same time I was excited. They were so... so manly, so earthy. You can't imagine the impression they make on a woman. And when we reached the camp and I met Black Buffalo Woman and began accustoming myself to things, when I found I could contribute and that they were willing to accept me I was so relieved. And..." She turned to look at him. "So proud of myself. They respected me as a person, which is more than Edgar ever did."

"It still woulda wound up in disaster for ya. For all the reasons you already know, reasons you really got nothin' t' do with. What you were doin' was jumpin' from the fryin' pan into the fire."

"You'll never convince me of that. Simply because you don't know me, you're not inside me, you don't feel what I feel. You have no idea what I need. What I crave."

He thought of the hapless He-Dog and the equally unlucky Standing Bear and wondered why it was that so many people who wanted things their way found they had to disrupt others' lives to achieve that. They hurt people to help themselves and most of the time didn't even realize what they were doing.

Nevertheless, he continued to feel sympathy for her, and that made him feel annoyed with himself. He'd been telling himself all along that he was just doing his job, doing the right thing. For her and for her husband. It was the accepted thing, certainly, but that didn't necessarily make it right. If it was so right why was it taking up housekeeping in his conscience? Taking over his conscience? He didn't think of himself as soft-hearted, but then Allan Pinkerton didn't think that way about himself, and yet he was, underneath the crust, behind the surliness and sarcasm. And what was wrong with a soft heart? Wasn't that one of the things that made human beings human rather than just beings?

Yes, he was annoyed with himself, and regret was beginning to set in as well. And they still had about twenty miles to go.

"What are you thinking about?" she asked. "Second thoughts about finishing the job, I hope."

"Nope."

Early in the afternoon they began to see signs of civilization, passing a couple of farm wagons and a carriage carrying an elderly couple. They waved a greeting as Raider and Adrienne drew closer.

"Oh God," she murmured, "now it starts."

"What?"

"It's the Griswolds. He manages the sawmill. They go to our church. He and Edgar are . . . Shhh!"

Raider smiled. He wasn't the one talking.

The old man was stopping his horse. Raider and Adrienne stopped. Mrs. Griswold gasped. "Heavenly days, it's you! Rescued! Oh gracious Lord! Thank Him and bless His name! Are you all right, my dear?"

"I'm fine, Ellen."

"You look exhausted."

"You look fine," corrected Mr. Griswold.

"Edgar's been beside himself," Mrs. Griswold went on, talking through her husband's words. "He'll be overjoyed, poor man. Oh gracious Lord, thank Him and bless His name, isn't this wonderful? A miracle!"

The Griswolds drove on and Raider and Adrienne resumed riding. An hour later they spotted a buckboard raising dust, heading toward Collardsville, about a half mile ahead. They caught up with it. Straw was liberally scattered about the bed, the tailgate flapped loose, the driver was so fat he took up most of the double seat. Raider recognized him while he was still about two hundred yards away.

"Meshach Gatling!" he burst.

The sheriff was overjoyed to see them. His round face broke into a smile that rivaled the brightness of the sun overhead.

"I'll be . . ."

Raider answered his every question when they stopped. He refastened the tailgate and tied both horses to it to trail behind. Adrienne collected the straw in the bed, lay down, and went to sleep. Raider squeezed in beside the sheriff.

"She looks okay," whispered Gatling.

"She is. I don't know how, but we made it."

"You wanna know something? I never did doubt for a second but what you'd pull it off. I have to tell you he did, her husband. He hired four misfits, promised 'em five hunnerd bucks apiece to go after her and bring her back."

"I know, we ran into them."

"What happened?"

"This and that, they run into a little bad luck; wound up dead."

"All four?" He whistled sharply, caught himself, turning to make sure he didn't wake her, turned back and asked with his eyes for elaboration.

"Injuns got 'em, them that was chasin' after her an' me."

"Did they . . . you know, abuse her?"

"Not really."

"What do you mean not really? They did or didn't."

"Nobody hurt her."

"How in the world did you manage it?"

"Lots o' luck, Meshach. I sneaked her out middle o' the night, rode like the wind." His hand sneaked around and under his seat. He winced. "We get back to Collardsville I'm gonna stand up for the next two days. Stand up on the friggin' train all the way back to Omaha or wherever. Brother, this has been one helluva two weeks."

"Nobody hurt her, you say. They just wouldn't let her go. That's strange. Why hang onto her if not to, you know..."

Raider lowered his voice. "Let me tell you somethin'. Strictly between you an' me. You gotta promise never tell a livin' soul. I'm only tellin' you on account you been straight with me from day one, helped me an' all."

"What, what?"

"Sssh. Chrissakes don't wake 'er up. She didn't want t' come back. She wanted t' take up livin' with 'em for keeps. Meshach, she liked it, she loved it."

"She found herself a boy friend."

"Bringin' 'er back has been like tryin' to pull a steer outta a bog, I swear, it's been murder!"

"So why did you?"

"Don't say that! I mean don't say that. . . . I don't know why. What am I sayin'? Course I do. 'Cause o' him, Edgar, and her. 'Cause it was my job to."

"Right."

"Whatta ya mean, 'right'?"

"Take it easy, I'm just agreein'. Lordy me, she gets herself kidnapped by Injuns, the last thing in the world you'd do is leave her with 'em, right?"

Raider didn't answer. He fixed his eyes on the road ahead and kept them there. He'd already said too much, he thought. He wasn't about to unburden his conscience, divulge his reservations about the thing, confess his regrets, admit that he was already having second thoughts about the whole thing. And that when he came face to face with Dubois he'd likely regret it thoroughly.

They'd been talking so long, plunging into a recapitulation of the events in the Black Hills, that until Raider looked up he had no idea how close they'd come to town. He could see houses and barns and presently the main street appeared. Halfway up it, on the left, stood the bank.

He pictured Edgar, sitting in his private office, working.

Pictured himself walking in, their eyes meeting. Damn, he didn't look forward to it, just imagining it triggered a queasy feeling. He glanced back at the sleeping woman.

Poor thing, he thought, why should he whine? It would be a lot harder on her than on him.

CHAPTER TWENTY FOUR

Ushered into Edgar Dubois' office, Raider was greeted with utter astonishment.

"You!"

"Can I sit?" Raider asked politely.

Edgar was looking behind him. A leer of triumph displaced his surprise.

"I see you didn't bring her back. Did you even find her? You obviously failed to, so what are you doing here? We have nothing to talk about. I don't want to be rude, but I'm a busy man..."

"Would you shut up a second? She's back, she's over t' Gatling's. She's okay, not hurt or nothin', just tired an' not all that happy t' be back. I see the good news is really gettin' t' you. Hey, you just gonna sit there or you goin' on over an' say hello, welcome home..."

"You really brought her back?"

"Whatta ya think, I'm pullin' your leg? Go see for yourself."

"In a minute. If, as you say, she's unharmed, she can keep for another few minutes; I mean she *has* been away two weeks. How the devil did you manage it?"

"D' you really care t' know? Jesus Christ, you are somethin'. Can't even get up off your ass and walk 'cross the street."

Edgar got up. "I'm going."

"What's that funny-lookin' thing on your face?"

"It's to protect my broken jaw."

"How'dja do that?"

"You did it, as if you didn't know! It may interest you to

know I'm considering suing the Agency and you personally." At the door he paused and turned. "Coming?"

"Don'cha want a little privacy?"

"Oh, very well. But you can't stay here."

"Okay, okay..."

They walked together through the bank to the street door, all eyes on the two of them. Edgar lowered his voice.

"You didn't happen to run into four men from town, did you?"

"They run into us, whatja do, empty out Gatling's drunk tank? Boy, you sure can pick 'em. If you're wonderin' what happened to 'em, wherever they are they're prob'ly wonderin', too. All four bought it."

"You killed them!"

"Ssssh, Chrissakes..."

"You discovered they were competing with you, that they were in my employ, and you brutally did away with them."

Raider told him what happened. They stood outside. From Edgar's face he clearly didn't believe a word he was hearing. If Raider had any doubt of it, his listener quickly dispelled it.

"That's the biggest cock and bull story I've ever heard. Of course you've had ample time to concoct it. Why don't I ask Adrienne? At least she can be truthful."

"Fuck you."

"You shut your foul mouth, don't you dare address me in such a fashion, you filthy tramp."

"Filthy I am..." He started off.

"Where are you going?"

"Over t' the hotel an' take a bath. It sure has been a pleasure seein' you again, Edgar ol' boy, you sure are a sight for sore eyes and a barrel o' laughs. It's been fun. I'll say good-bye."

"Wait..."

"What for? Everythin's come out in the wash, it's all over, happy ending, you two lovebirds reunited, case closed. And this really is so long, I'm catchin' the first train outta this hole and never comin' back."

"That's good news."

Raider walked off about six paces, then turned to face him. Now he came back two steps.

"Better for me, wiseass. I only got one last thing t' say t' you. You be good t' that little girl, you snob sonovabitch. Treat 'er like a woman, like the wife she is, stop pissin' on 'er like you do everybody else. She's been through six kinds o' hell..."

"You think it's been easy on me? Do you?"

"Easy as hell. Why not? You got no more feelin' for her than you do for yesterday's breakfast." He softened his tone into appeal. "Just be good t' her, please. She'll need time t' throw it off her. It's like she's come through a major op'ration and has t'... you know... recup'rate, recover. She's gonna have nightmares the rest o' her days. Be gentle, Edgar, be kindly."

Edgar stared through him.

"If you're quite finished, I must say I do think I'm capable of conducting myself humanely. I'm neither insensitive nor unresponsive. Indeed, I happen to prize my capacity for compassion. And I think I do know how to talk to my own wife! Good day and good riddance."

"Same t' you with feathers on it," muttered Raider walking away.

Raider made straight for the railroad station, electing to postpone his bath and his date with a bottle. He couldn't wait to get out of town.

"You got about a two-hour wait for the six-eighteen down to Bridgeport. Change there to the Union Pacific. It'll take you straight through to Omaha," said the wiry little man in a vest and boiled shirt with a green visor shading his rheumy eyes, his bald pate lifting above it like an inverted bowl.

"Jesus, you mean t' say there's no train till six-eighteen? What kinda damn railroad you got here, anyways?"

"Not a very good one, but this is Collardsville, not Omaha or New York. Can't you find some way to kill two little hours?"

"Not in this burg."

"You could go take a bath."

"Mind your own beeswax, Pop!"

"Sorry, I just meant you do look like you been pushed through a feed cutter. You feelin' okay?"

"Aces, don't I look it?"

"You always so grouchy?"

"Always. Gimme the damn ticket!"

Edgar strolled into Meshach Gatlin's office to find the sheriff and Adrienne talking. At sight of her husband she stood up. Gatling struggled to extricate his bulk from his chair.

"Don't go, Meshash," she said hurriedly.

"Please go," piped Edgar. "There's a good fellow, give us a little privacy."

"I'm goin', I'm goin'. Up the street and wet my whistle."

He closed the door after himself. She sank back down on the stool.

"You're looking well, Edgar . . . dear," she said quietly.

"Forget me, my dear, I'm not the one who's been doing the suffering, although I must say it hasn't been easy for me. Far from it. It's the nights especially. Forget sleep. I lay there night after night worrying, wondering."

"It must have been very trying for you."

"I'd be fibbing if I said it wasn't, and doubly hard on you, I'm sure. Do spare me the gorier details, but see here, Adrienne, I must be frank."

"About what?"

"This, your being abducted. It was very thoughtless of you to go wandering out there unescorted to pick berries. Couldn't you have asked one of your friends to go along? Astrid Montgomery carries a gun. You like Astrid, she would have gone. I don't like to carp, after all it is water over the dam, but to go out there all by yourself . . . my dear, it was childish."

"I'm sorry, Edgar."

"I know. I won't mention it again, I promise. Oh, did they hurt you?"

"No one hurt me."

"You've a bruise on your jaw." He remembered his own jaw, his hand went to it. "Raider struck me and broke mine. Without warning, without any provocation, the filthy scum. I do so detest and despise that man! Did he ... did he treat you respectfully?"

"Do you mean did he rape me?"

"Adrienne!"

"He was a perfect gentleman."

"Ha ha, that's rich, it boggles the mind."

"I mean it. You should be praising him, showering him with gratitude. He risked his life again and again. He's the most courageous man I've ever seen. If anybody else came to rescue me, they never would have succeeded. He's one in a million."

"Is he really? My my my, he certainly seems to have impressed you more than favorably."

She glared at him. Although he failed to notice it, the little patience she was able to engender for him had now given out, dispatched by his obtuseness.

"What is that supposed to mean?" she asked.

"Not a blessed thing, my dear, should it mean something?"

"You tell me."

He snickered. "Nothing. Of course you two *were* out there together some time..."

"I'm sorry, Edgar. But not for you, unfortunately, you and your sordid mind. I'm sorry I came back. I see now I should have kept going down to the depot. And boarded the first train out of here. It's not going to work, is it? It's not possible; we'll only be wasting our time."

"Don't talk nonsense. Of course it's possible. It may sound absurd, but I see a good side to all of this, bad as it was. It separated us for two full weeks. I've had a lot of time to think about you, my dear, and our marriage. I'm sure you have, too. Thought about your mistakes, how you would do things if you had them to do over, that sort of thing. I've thought about my part in our marriage. I'm not averse to recognizing my good points, and I'm sure I must have some bad. Nobody's perfect."

"I'm very tired, Edgar, can we postpone discussing it until later? I want to go home, take a hot bath, go to bed and sleep away the next two days."

"Of course. I understand."

She searched his eyes. Her own seemed to say "I only wish you could," but she did not put the look into words.

CHAPTER TWENTY FIVE

Raider repaired to his old hotel room, ordered up a bath and immersed himself in water so hot it turned his skin as pink as a ripe peach. After he had finished soaping down, he lay in the tub and relaxed, piecing together the events of the past two weeks in chronological order. He didn't find it particularly enjoyable, but thoughts of the Indians, the soldiers, Amory, the Hotalings, and of his own many close calls did keep her out of his mind. Until he was brought up to the moment.

He groaned. For her. Picturing the happy couple's reunion. Despite his warning to Edgar he'd no doubt lay her out in lavender for going out berrying alone, not even bringing a gun along; that would start them arguing, at that very moment they were probably barking at each other.

"Like two mutts..."

He retrieved the bar of soap from the floor, soaped up his chest, and resumed scrubbing himself, taking pains to avoid his rib wound. As he'd anticipated, he was feeling even sorrier for her now than he had when he'd walked away from Edgar in the street. He decided he would go see her one last time before leaving town.

Ten minutes later, with still more than an hour before train time, he walked into Meshach Gatling's office. The sheriff was alone, sitting surrounded by his favorite chair, playing his harmonica. He took it down, rapping the spit out of it against his palm at sight of his visitor.

"Well you sure look like a changed man. Shave and all."

"Where are they?"

Gatling leered. "Who might that be?"

"Cut the clowning."

"King Edgar's gone back to work. She went home. I was on my way back here from up the street, I saw her headin' that way. Why?"

"Where's the house?"

"Down the end of the street and turn left. Second house on your left. Big white frame, yellow roses on the trellises, you can't miss it. Why? You going to say good-bye?"

"Thanks."

Raider shook his hand.

"When you leavin' town?" Gatling asked.

"About an hour."

"It's been a gen-oo-ine pleasure, Mr. Pinkerton."

"Same here. Take care, don' go steppin' on any more bankers' insteps. So long."

She answered the door knocker in nightdress and dressing gown. Her hair was pinned up. She had cleaned up. She looked exhausted; she looked beautiful. So beautiful that it momentarily took away his breath. She'd been asleep.

"I woke you..."

"It's all right."

"I'm sorry. I'm leavin' on the six-eighteen, I just wanted to say good-bye."

It sounded so lame, he thought, so stupid. He suddenly felt stupid. Not knowing what to do with his hands, shifting his feet, trying—and failing—to avoid her eyes.

"Come in." She smiled as she said it and stood aside. he hesitated. "Please, just for a few minutes."

"That's 'bout all I can spare."

She closed the door behind him and gestured him to a chair in the parlor. She sat opposite him. It was very homey and smelled faintly of orange blossoms, *some* perfume he could not identify. The tasseled furniture looked expensive. Stern looking men stared out of wooden frames on the walls. One of them had to be Edgar's father, he thought, it was hard to tell which, all bore a vague resemblence to each other. There were fresh flowers in a tall ugly vase on the table by the front window: yellow roses. He wanted to ask her *the* question, but his curiosity could not get up the gumption to. She rescued him. She smiled weakly.

"You're dying to know how it went."

"It's none o' my bus'ness."

"How do you think?"

"How would I know?"

"You're a card, Raider, you've so much of the little boy in you, and yet you're all man. That doesn't make sense, does it? It went exactly as you imagine it did. We ended up arguing. The whole mess was my fault of course, somehow I knew it would be. We promised to give the farce that he calls our marriage another try. Yet another. I promised."

"Are you gonna?"

"I suppose. I don't see as I have much choice, do you?"

"You got a choice. And you sure see it, only it'll take guts t' take it."

"Get dressed, pack my things, go over to the bank and say good-bye, and get on your train with you, right?"

"There's allus another train. Just like there's allus a choice. Sometimes you gotta take the bull by the horns like they say."

"Mmmmm. Whenever I hear that expression I can't help wonder if 'they' ever do. Would you like some tea?"

"No thanks."

They sat staring at each other. She tilted her head to one side and gave him a lovely smile, one that forgave him everything, that conveyed gratitude and appreciation, admiration, fondness, all gathered in a single expression. He smiled in return, lowered his head, and resumed turning his hat brim in his hand. Then he got up.

"I better be going."

"A few more minutes? Just a couple."

"I should go."

"You surprise me. This is as hard for you as it is for me. No, I'm not surprised. You never did muster any real resentment toward me, you always worried, always cared."

She laughed lightly. "Even when you were knocking me out." She rubbed her chin. The bruise was very light, but distinguishable.

They shook hands. She saw him out. At the door she pulled him down and kissed him lingeringly on the cheek.

"Good-bye, Raider."

"Good-bye, Adrienne."

CHAPTER TWENTY SIX

Raider wired headquarters in Chicago when he arrived in Omaha. A response came two hours later. He was ordered to board a train for Chicago. The following afternoon he walked into William Wagner's office. The superintendent's jaw dropped and his broad face broke into a smile, his cigar butt dropping from his mouth, bouncing on his desk. He quickly restored it.

"Rade!"

"Whatcha lookin' so s'prised for, you ordered me t' come, Chrissakes."

"Sit, sit. Congratulations, good job, superb. I understand it turned out hairier than usual. The chief tells me you were lucky to get out of it alive."

"I don't know where he got that. Oh, I sent in my case report, but I di'n't make myself out no hero. That's not my style."

"He didn't get if from your report; it was somebody in Collardsville. They sent him a long telegram, chapter and verse. I think it was the sheriff. Gatling?"

"Meshach Gatling. Nice fella', only a bullshit artist."

"Modesty, modesty. Is something wrong, Rade?"

"Why you ask me that?"

"You look even more sour than usual. Something happen out there you didn't include in your report? You can confide in me, I won't tell the chief."

"Mr. Wagner, from start t' finish the whole thing stunk t' high heaven. She, Mrs. Dubois, got herself snatched, they took her back t' the main tribe an' what does she do but fall in love with ever'body. Why? How could such a thing happen? Simple. She can't stand her husband. Chrissakes, if she was carried off by friggin' jungle gorillas she's prefer 'em t' him."

"Edgar..."

"The man is the biggest asshole in creation. I never met one like 'im. Two minutes with 'im an' you wanna throw up, so help me. We hated each other from the git-go."

"It all worked out."

"Because he wasn't round to screw things up."

"That reminds me, he's suing the Agency and you for your breaking his jaw."

"Fuck 'im."

"Oh, he won't get to first base. The chief's already discussed it with the lawyers. We all take it for granted he provoked you; Mr. Pinkerton certainly does. Besides, in most minor assault cases when things get down to particulars, the plaintiff usually drops the charge. Given a little time to calm down and view the thing objectively, he usually decides pursuing it is more trouble than it's worth."

"I don't care what the hell he does. She's the only one that counts."

The door flew open and Pinkerton came striding in.

"Raider, Raider, Raider, my boy you're sight for sore eyes. It's good to see you! Guess why I brought you back here? Guess."

"I dunno, you got a medal you wanna pin on me? A big fat raise?"

The chief laid a fatherly hand on his shoulder, grinned and addressed Wagner.

"What a sense of humor this lad has! Priceless! No, my boy, better than either and no one deserves it more! Starting tomorrow morning you're going on two weeks vacation. Paid vacation. You want to go to bed for two weeks and drink yourself insensible, do it! You want to go to bed and dally with some diseased woman of the streets, do it! You want to go sailing on Lake Michigan..."

"All right, All right... what you're really sayin' is, no raise."

Pinkerton's reaction was one of acute pain. His hand drifted to his heart.

"They're all the same, William, aren't they? Mercenary to the core." He shook his head in mock despair.

A knock sounded. It was Alan Pinkerton's secretary.

"You remember Operative Raider..." gushed the chief.

They nodded to each other.

"Telegram just came in, sir."

She gave it to him, he thanked her, she vanished, leaving Raider her most motherly smile. The chief read the yellow paper.

"My soul and body..." he murmured and sank into the chair. Then he recovered and handed the telegram to Raider.

"Who's it from?" inquired Wagner.

"Harmon Dubois, the boy's father."

Raider was reading:

...REGRET TO INFORM YOU TRAGEDY HAS STRUCK STOP THIS MORNING APPROXIMATELY SIX THIRTY DAUGHTER IN LAW ADRIENNE TOOK HER OWN LIFE STOP HUSBAND EDGAR DISTRAUGHT STOP HE FOUND HER STOP AM ON MY WAY COLLARDSVILLE STOP WILL KEEP YOU APPRISED STOP THE DARLING CHILD STOP MY OWN HEART IS BROKEN

HD

Raider crumpled the telegram and dropped it on the floor. Both men's eyes were fastened on him, but he did not look at either. Instead he rose slowly from his chair, turned to the wall, and hammered it with his fist as hard as he could swing.

"Owwwwwww!"

They rushed to him. Wagner examined his fist. The chief examined the wall.

"You've broken it!" Pinkerton burst.

"Broken his hand, too," said Wagner.

Raider withdrew it from his gentle grasp. "Fuck it."

"But why?"

Raider shrugged. He seemed to be effectively ignoring the pain. "Couldn't help myself. You boys wouldn' unnerstand. Nobody would, nobody in the whole world. 'Cept her, she'd unnerstand. Hey Wagner, you got any booze in that funny lookin' desk? Anything'll do, 'cept rye. It makes me sick."

The hard-hitting, gun-slinging Pride of the Pinkertons is riding solo in this new action-packed series.

J.D. HARDIN'S
RAIDER

Sharpshooting Pinkertons Doc and Raider are legends in their own time, taking care of outlaws that the local sheriffs can't handle. Doc has decided to settle down and now Raider takes on the nastiest vermin the Old West has to offer single-handedly...charming the ladies along the way

__0-425-11057-5	**BAJA DIABLO #15**	$2.95
__0-425-11105-9	**STAGECOACH RANSOM #16**	$2.95
__0-425-11195-4	**RIVERBOAT GOLD #17**	$2.95
__0-425-11266-7	**WILDERNESS MANHUNT #18**	$2.95
__0-425-11315-9	**SINS OF THE GUNSLINGER #19**	$2.95

Please send the titles I've checked above. Mail orders to:

BERKLEY PUBLISHING GROUP
390 Murray Hill Pkwy., Dept. B
East Rutherford, NJ 07073

NAME_____
ADDRESS_____
CITY_____
STATE_____ ZIP_____

Please allow 6 weeks for delivery.
Prices are subject to change without notice.

POSTAGE & HANDLING:
$1.00 for one book, $.25 for each additional. Do not exceed $3.50.

BOOK TOTAL $_____
SHIPPING & HANDLING $_____
APPLICABLE SALES TAX $_____
(CA, NJ, NY, PA)
TOTAL AMOUNT DUE $_____
PAYABLE IN US FUNDS.
(No cash orders accepted.)